Maid to Kill

Maid to Kill

by

Gregory Walker

1stBooks - rev. 01/26/00

About the Book

A humble, lonely but obsessive black maid is hired by a black corporate executive and his young, pretty, white wife. As time progresses, the maid plots to break up the marriage out of her jealousy of a successful black man being married to a white woman, but it backfires. The maid is subjected to much degradation and humiliation by the young, white female. But, the maid, who has four children, cannot afford to quite because they are paying her well and she has limited job skills.

Finally, in the heat of passion, a fight breaks out and the maid kills the young, white female and buries her in the backyard. The black executive is devastated by his wife's disappearance and begins to drink heavily. One night after consuming much liquor, he awakes with the maid cuddled under him from a romantic encounter. Later, he awakes again from dogs making noise in his backyard. When he investigates, he finds a hand with a ring on it, the one he gave his wife on their wedding day.

CHAPTER ONE--We Need A Maid

My name is Henry Arture Cook. I am a 40-year-old black man. My father was a chef at a Holiday Inn and my mother was a maid in the household of Mr. Townsend who owned a 200-acre farm in Mississippi. My wife Gina, who is 24 years old and a beautiful blonde with hazel eyes, and I have been married now for three years.

We moved to Georgia in 1993. She likes it there because she likes to garden her precious roses. I work as a senior executive for a major corporation -- being the first black to break the barrier on that level. My wife constantly complains about all the housework she has to do and with the income that I make she feels like we could afford to hire a maid. We would argue day and night, day in and day out, on this issue until I finally gave in and we hired Miss Betsy, a black lady about 37 years old. Miss Betsy was poor and badly needed the job and income to take care of her family because her husband had passed away from cancer. Miss Betsy was very colorful and always joyous in her work but I sensed a little jealousy that she felt because I had a white wife. As time progressed I could see a change in the way Gina and her got along, the tension and resentment and Miss Betsy biting her mouth at the right moment to protect her job security.

5:00 A.M. Saturday

After a long night of lovemaking between me and my wife I could hear someone weeping but I had no idea who it could be. Then it came to mind that Miss Betsy's room was parallel to our bedroom. She had slept overnight to cook breakfast in the morning; her four children were kept by her mother. I rolled over and looked at Gina. She was asleep lying on her stomach; I caressed her back down to her bottom, halfway awake she gazed into my eyes passionately and sighed. I could still smell the wine from last night along with her youthful baby breath. I heard a sizzling noise and the aroma of bacon and someone singing.

I knew Miss Betsy was preparing breakfast so I called Miss Betsy! "Could you serve us in bed?"

"Yes sir, Mr. Cook!" She said, coming up seconds later. She opened the door and opened a small table near our bed. She glanced up at Gina who had on a sexy black lingerie bikini, I could see the hurt in her eyes but I pretended not too. There she stood hesitantly and murmured, "I will be right back sir with your breakfast. I cook your eggs just the way you like 'em, sunny-side-up." I elbowed Gina lightly in the rib and woke her up.

She looked at me and I said, "time to eat breakfast."

She looked at me and said, "you are my breakfast," and she bit me playfully on the arm. When Miss Betsy returned, Gina sat up on the bed.

I asked Miss Betsy, "why were you crying?"

She said, "I was thinking about my husband and how much I miss him and the hard time I am having trying to raise up my kids right."

"Yea, that must be hard." I said.

Gina said, "everything will be alright."

Miss Betsy said, "I hope so and I pray every day to the Good Lord. How do you want your coffee, Mr. Cook?" she asked. "You know sometime you drink your coffee black and sometime with a lot of cream and sugar."

"I want it black this morning Miss Betsy."

"And you Miss Gina, how do you want yours?" she asked.

"I just want some milk," Gina said.

"I think I am going to wear my money green Irish plaid suit today when I meet the guys for our weekly Saturday noon pool tournament."

"I think that looks very nice on you dear. I will tell Betsy to get it ready," Gina said, as she got out of bed and looked at herself in the mirror.

I looked at her, grabbed her hand and pulled her to the bed; then gave her a deep soulful kiss when Miss Betsy entered, "I got your break-" She stopped, and laid it on the table and walked out. As the door closed she had her fist to her mouth biting with her teeth tearfully as it was tearing her apart to see what she had just witnessed between me and Gina, unbeknownst to me at the time.

12 noon had arrived and I was at Speeds Billiards with my best friends Ralph, Arnold and some other guys. Ralph aimed to shoot and asked, "How are you and Gina?"

"We're doing Ok; I guess."

"I heard you got a maid." He shoots and makes a ball and walks around the table. "How is that working out?" He asks.

"Aaah, it's alright."

Arnold looks at me, smiles and asks, "is she pretty?"

"No."

"She an older lady? Oh, around your age." Arnold says and laughs.

"You keep talking and you won't be around to reach my age."

"You better pay attention to the game he's kicking your butt," Arnold says.

Later as I returned home, I could see my wife watering her roses outside as I approach the house in my car. She looked very nice in her calico design print dress. I kissed her on the neck as I walked toward the door as I entered I saw Betsy on the phone listening to some music. "Hello, Mr. Cook," said Betsy. "How was your pool game today sir?"

"It was Ok. Hey, did anyone call for me? I am supposed to go out of town Monday to Pittsburgh for a seminar."

"No sir, not that I know of," she said, with her hand over the telephone.

"Your boyfriend?" I pointed at the phone.

"Naw sir, just a friend," she said. Her mind began to think that I had an interest because I asked but in reality I wished that she would find someone stable and willing to help her out in her current financial situation. She hung up the phone and followed me to the living-room and asked, "Sir I don't mean no disrespect but why you marry a white woman, couldn't you find a black woman that was worthwhile?"

I turned around and looked at her agitated and upset as she stood there humbly not meaning any harm but just curious. I was softened because she asked with the correct demeanor. I explain to her that Gina was a nice pretty girl, a rare find in any race, anywhere in the world and I know because I have traveled the world and know.

"No black woman anywhere was good enough?" she asked, as Gina entered I was just going to answer but stopped.

Gina asked, "what's going on?"

"Nothing," I said.

Gina looked at me and smiled and told Betsy, "could you leave us alone for a little while? Like go to your room and shut the door?"

Miss Betsy was hurt as she, with her head down walked slowly to her room. Gina hugged me, "I want to make love to you right here and now in the living-room on the couch."

Betsy looked back and heard this and saw us carrying on and then entered her room. She untied her maids' uniform and sat on her bed. "Lord, tell me why these black men now days go after these white women? All us sisters can't even find a decent man anywhere." Now she hears the sounds of passionate love making, Gina panting loud and calling my name. Betsy grabs a pillow and lies down and puts it over her ears so she doesn't have to listen.

An hour later Betsy hears her name being called by Gina, she comes in and sees Gina now wearing shorts and I was in a robe in bed. Gina points at the towels on the floor, "could you wash those right away?" she said.

"Yes, ma'am." As Betsy picked up the towels, our underwear fell to the carpet.

"Oh yea . . . that too" said Gina. "They were soiled from our encounter previously."

Betsy took it and left disgusted, then mumbled under her breath.

"I am so glad we have a maid Henry. You see how much more sexual I can be with you now that I am not tired from doing housework all day?" said Gina.

"Oh yes, just like it was when we first started seeing each other. I really wish that Betsy would get a boyfriend. Do you know what she asked me today?"

"No what?" said Gina.

"She asked me why I married a white girl. You know how these black women are when they see a successful black man with a white woman. When I was single and struggling, I couldn't find a black woman anywhere who would give me a nickel worth of time. They think they are worth money just to be with them but don't know how to be beside a gifted black man and help him achieve."

"Don't worry about that dear," said Gina.

"They don't even understand how to be a woman most of them," I said.

"Maybe we can get somebody else dear," said Gina.

"No, I don't want to kick her out in the cold without anything."

"I don't like to see you upset like this," said Gina.

"Yea," I said sarcastically. She softly grabs my arm, rolls me over and says, "let me rub your back to relieve some

to be purple and you are going to need a wheel to get around in. You ever heard of Clarence Carter song, I'm stroking?"
"No," Gina said.
"You want me to sing it?"
She laughs, "yea."
I begin to sing . . .

> I'm stroking, I'm stroking
> I'm stroking to the east
> I'm stroking to the west
> I'm stroking to the one
> that I love the best, I'm stroking
> and when it gets good
> she starts to say my name
> Clarence Carter, Clarence Carter

"That's enough," she laughs and hits me on the arm. She asks, "where did that song come from?"
"That was a hit from the 70's. You never heard that before?"
"I bet you Miss Betsy is stroking right now with somebody," said Gina.
"That's no concern of mine. Let me recite to you a poem I wrote." I took Gina's hand.

> Near the valley there is a river
> which runs smooth and quiet to the sea
> that stimulates my inner passion
> when you are here with me
> I never love someone so true and deeply
> with all my heart completely
>
> when I look into your eyes
> I see innocence and sweetness

captured by your wonderful love
My only life weakness.

"Do you like it?"

"Yes," said Gina. She looked at me and went to the closet and start searching through her clothes. "I wonder where my red lace panties are," she said.

"Oh, I love those. Hey, why do you hang panties on a hanger anyway?"

"Do you want to see me in wrinkled panties?" she asked.

* * * * *

At the same time Betsy is waiting on a bus stop. She sees a few black men hanging out by a liquor store with beer bottles in their hands, talking and cursing and swearing very loud with laughter. She bows her head and begins to pray for them. 'My Father who art in heaven, etc.' Later a black man, in a black suit with a dog, walks up to her and sits beside her.

She looks at the dog and says, "at least it's not a white woman."

The man looked at her and said, "my woman is at home cooking dinner." He did not however, say what color she was and Betsy looked at him and murmured, 'another black man with a white girl.'

Annoyed he looked at her and said, "no, I was in the Navy for 10 years and my wife I met while I was in Japan, she's Japanese. He went into a long story. You see, my mother only educated my sisters and didn't care about any of my brothers or me getting education beyond high school. We had to leave the house once we became 18 years old, not even fully equipped for the racism that we were going to endure for being a black man. The thing is . . . once Martin Luther King, Jr. won civil rights for the black race the black woman, our

8

mothers, undermined the black male by hurting her own flesh and blood with sexism that's why you see these black men everywhere in every city with a backpack on their back."

Miss Betsy just looked at him in silence and anger. "These black men are just lazy and don't want to work," she said.

"These black men were skillfully cheated and manipulated by their mothers to make them think that being intelligent and being a black man was not okay, which is just as bad as what the white people has done to us. I made it because I was determined and could not see myself being nothing," he said.

Betsy stands angry, "let me tell you something. I work for a black man with a white wife who treats me like a child and I have to clean their dirty underwear after they have sex," she said.

The man stands, begins to walk away then looks back. "Maybe you should have made something out of yourself and stop looking at other people blaming them for your misfortunes in life," he said.

"Shut up, shut up!" Betsy screams. She bends down to pick up a rock.

"You hit me with that rock and I will call the police," the man said.

Betsy, thinking about her kids best interest drops the rock.

The man begins to sing . . .

> Nobody's fault but mine
> if I don't get to heaven
> it ain't nobody's fault but mine
> nobody's fault but mine
> nobody's fault but mine
> if I don't get to heaven
> it ain't nobody's fault but mine

When the bus pulled up Miss Betsy gets on and sits. The lady beside her sees she is upset, "are you alright?" she asks.

"Yes, I'm fine, thank you," Betsy says and smiles. After a long bus ride Miss Betsy finally arrives home and is greeted inside by her kids and mother.

"Child I didn't think you would ever come home," her mother said.

Her two 6-year-old twin boys are draped around her legs because they are glad to see her.

"Mama, they really had me going." She stops and looks down. "Now, you boys go over and sit over there by your sister, you see how nice and quiet they are over there," said Betsy.

"Those boys been sitting around with their lips stuck out ever since last night waiting for you to get home but finally they went to sleep," her mother said.

"They know I got to work to put food on the table and clothes on their backs," Betsy says.

"That's not what it is girl, they need you and what you need to do is find a man," her mama said.

"Don't nobody want a 37-year-old woman with four kids," Betsy said.

"Girl, you still young and pretty shoot, what you talking about?" her Mama said

"You just say that because I look like you," Betsy said.

"I'm pretty too . . . might be 50 . . . but I am a pretty granny," Mama says and laughs.

"All these men now days want white girls just like the brother I work for. You know every time a black man make a little money he goes and gets a white girl," said Betsy.

"That sure is true. They say men like that have a mother was mean to them," Mama said.

"That what the problem is?" asked Betsy.

"Yea girl, That's what it is or they are some kind of sex

freak in some kind of way," Mama said.

"I saw her choking him and on top of him like they were having sex," Betsy said.

See told her, "don't let that mess bother you honey," Mama said.

"So, he like for his woman to choke him," Betsy said.

"You boys better not grow up and mess with no white girls, we ain't gonna claim you no more if you do, you hear?" Mama said. They looked at her.

8:00 A.M. Sunday

Miss Betsy is in the kitchen cooking breakfast and Gina and I are seated in the dining room. "Gina, you know we have five bedrooms in this house and no one to occupy them. I was thinking about maybe renting them out to some college students."

"I think they would be a little too noisy," Gina said.

"Well of course, we have to rent to the right people to avoid that. Probably leaning more toward the introvert personality type of person or a computer wiz."

"Maybe we could let Miss Betsy bring her kids on the weekend to be with her and they can use the rooms. You know how lonely she looks sometimes," Gina said.

"I think that's a good idea."

Miss Betsy enters with their breakfast, "here's your toast, your eggs, your sausage, bacon and hash browns. Is there anything else I can get you this morning?" Betsy asked.

"We want to make you an offer," Gina said.

"Would you like to bring your children with you here on the weekends? We have four unoccupied bedrooms," I asked.

Miss Betsy smiled, "you really mean that sir?" she asked.

"I think it would be fun to have some children around to liven-up the place, we still working on having our own," Gina said.

"Yes, you can bring them with you starting next Saturday."

CHAPTER TWO--Trouble Waters

I was over Arnold's house. He wanted me to listen to him read an essay he had written about white people and their adverse effect on humanity as a whole.

Sitting on his couch; he stood before me with papers in his hand. He smiled, "I am not talking about you or what you do, this is just an essay from my point of view," he said.

"It's okay with me just read, I'll be quiet and give you my opinion after you are through."

"All white people are innately algolagnia; they enjoy the pain and suffering of others especially those of another race. Some white people tend to be attractive but the ones who lack physical beauty or mental talents seem to be most likely to be algolagnia. As a people they seem to be very close even when they hate one another. There is no real devised structure on their social interactions however, the individual or individuals they view as weak or different are on the bottom of their hierarchy. They are quick to become racist because of this fact. Their socialization with other races is to be supple, cunning and subversive when their actual goal is to steal, divide and assimilate and use them to comfort those of their race who have a vast amount of pathologies thus boosting their false belief of supremacy because they are catered to by those who sympathize with them."

Arnold continued by this time I had stopped listening to them and retreated into my own world.

"Okay, now tell me what you think about that," Arnold asked.

"How can you substantiate any of that what you just said?" I asked.

"It's all around you man, can't you see?" he said.

"I don't believe all of that is true, maybe some parts but come on man. People are going to think you are the next Louis Fakkhan," I said.

"I don't care what people think someone out there shares my views," he said.

"Well, I am going to be going home now," I said and started walking toward the door.

"Hey, see you Saturday for our noon match at pool," he said.

"Sure," I said, and exited out his door and it was a nice sunny day about 70 degrees. As I walked down the street, I could see some children laughing and playing basketball on a nearby court. There were some little girls skipping rope and I begin feeling lonely about having some children of my own. Gina and I are going to have to get to work on children, I thought to myself. Finally I made it home and I saw Betsy outside sweeping the walkway to the house.

"Good evening, Mr. Cook," she said.

"Good evening Betsy. How are you today?" I asked.

"I am fine, thank you," she said.

"Hey, is Gina inside?" I asked.

"Yes sir, she inside," Betsy said. Betsy looked at me wantonly as I walked up the stairs to the door. I turned around and looked at her for a moment and went inside. Gina is watching TV and deeply into whatever is on.

"Hey, are we not on speaking terms?" I ask jokingly.

"No, it's not that," she replied.

"What are you looking at anyway?" I asked. I walk over and its one of those talk shows with a guy wearing lingerie who likes to dress like a woman. "Why are you watching this?" I asked.

"I just think it's weird because I never heard of it before," she said.

"I'm never going to wear your panties so don't get any

ideas," I said.

She laughs. Miss Betsy enters and looks at the TV. Seeing what is going on, she looks at me and Gina. "Don't you have something else to do Betsy?" Gina asks.

"Yes ma'am," says Betsy and she walks out.

"I was over Arnold's house and he read me his essay. `Things you should know about white people' or something like that. Anyway parts of it read that the reason why white people interracial-marry is to heal their pathologies of low self-esteem. We are together because we are from the same economical and social level. I don't know who he can be talking about. I can't remember everything he said but it will come back to me," I said.

"I am not really interested in what Arnold has to say. You know Arnold don't like me or anybody else white," Gina said.

"Arnold is still young and has not traveled alot in the world and experienced different races and cultures. It would open up his mind some if he did. He's probably talking about me behind my back, calling me an uncle Tom or something. I think I am going to go take a shower," I said.

Later as I was walking into the bathroom, I saw Betsy looking at me wrapped in a towel with my muscled chest showing. "Mr. Cook, is there anything I can do for you?" Betsy asked.

It seems to be quite divisive question and could be interpreted as a slight come on as her eyes said the rest along with her body language. "No," I said. "I'll do just fine; I continued. I walked into the shower and turned on the water."

Gina walked down the hall and past Betsy and saw her smiling and she wondered what the smile was for.

Miss Betsy went to her room trying to think of a reason to get a glimpse of me in the nude.

Finally she decides she would play like she forgot I was in the shower routine and with that she opened the door abruptly just as I was getting out of the shower without any clothes on or a towel around my body. Her eyes widened and mouth dropped as she witnessed the sight of my large endowment. I looked at her for a moment and told her to get out. She closed the door quickly and returned to her room running down the hall.

Gina came seconds later not knowing what had just happened. "Could you dry off my back?" I asked.

"Yea sure," she said.

"Gina, what are we going to do tonight I am bored?" I asked.

"I will think of something," she said.

At the same time Miss Betsy is in her room with a smile fantasizing about being with me and making love to me. She just wanted to give in and be taken strong and rough by me to make her feel small and weak. She closed her eyes and began to think of me for it has been such a long time since Miss Betsy has slept with anyone and her hand became active fondling her womanly lust. After a period of self gratifications she finally reached her climax and let out a faint of relief spent her from self arousal.

I was just tying my shoe and looked up at Gina and told her I was going to go to the bar for a while and have a few drinks.

"Don't go home with no one, especially a woman," said Gina.

"Get out of here girl, you know that you are the only one," I said.

"Drinking loosens your inhibitions and your mind opens to persuasion," she said.

"I'm forty years old," I said.

"You look twenty-seven not forty so don't pull that one on me," she said with a smile.

I exit out the door and it was still sunny and nice outside

around 6:30pm. I could hear the birds singing in a big Formosa tree and the swell of honeysuckles intoxicated my senses as a slight wind crossed my way. It wasn't a cloud in the sky on this particular day. I passed by Ralphs' house. I could see him in the backyard washing his car. His kids were playing in the front yard with a water hose running around and squirting each other with it. Ralph saw me and waved and I waved back and pointed at the neighborhood bar at the corner of the street.

He smiled and gave me a thumbs up and continued to wash his car. I remember ten years ago when I was single and trying to pickup black women, they used to talk about me because I liked to drink beer and go out. They did not consider me a stable, decent man because of that but little did they know that all a man need in his life is just someone who loves him to change his life around but the ones I met where way to shallow to ever conceive this notion. Then once I met Gina, they spread rumors that I was gay and they never saw me with a woman. True, none of them ever wanted me but the gay part is false and Gina did not believe them anyway. She could see that I was just lonely and searching for true love and that is why we are together today. Finally making it to the bar I enter and look around, its only about seven people inside and a few guys playing pool. I went and sat at the bar and the bartender asked me, "what do you want?"

I answer, "just a Budweiser."

He poured a tap and slide it down the bar to me and it stopped right in front of me. "I only saw that in the movies." He did not answer me he just turned around and started back doing whatever he was doing before I ordered. Later as I had downed a few beers I was in the mood to hear a little music so I went over to the jukebox and played some George Clinton, Barry White and Michael Jackson. Soon after I sat down and the music begins to play a big guy at the end of bar said, "whoever played this bullshit, I'm gonna kick his ass." His girlfriend who was sitting beside him pointed at me and I looked down not wanting to fight this man. He came over to me and asked, "are you the fag who played this?" he asked.

"Look; I don't want to fight you. Can I buy you a beer and let's forget about this?"

He said very angrily, "No!" as trickles of spit hit me in the face.

I stood up and hit him square on the chin and he was out cold. "You should have let me buy you a beer," and I sat back down. The bartender walked around and grabbed the man by the boots, dragged him outside in the alley and left him with his girlfriend following. She turned and looked at me and said, "you just don't know what you have done."

When they exited everyone at the bar clapped and yelled, "We are sick of his shit."

I really wasn't enjoying myself any more and I decided to go home and eat supper. It was now around 9pm. I could see every star in the sky as I looked above and could hear crickets and the sounds of night. Meanwhile at home Gina was trying on some of her knew dresses she had brought and was looking at herself in the mirror. "This looks a little too short," she said.

I rang the doorbell and she came and opened it. I looked at her in that short sexy dress and was turned on right away. "What are you wearing underneath? Nothing I hope."

"Why don't we go to the bedroom and find out?" she said.

With that I followed her unbuttoning my shirt and loosening my belt. At the same time at Miss Betsy house she was talking to her mother. "Mama, I'm so tired today."

"Ain't nothing wrong with you, except you need a man, and you would be up and dancing around with your heart singing inside," she said.

"I can't find no-good man, Mama. They all taken," Betsy

said.

"It bound to be one man out there for you somewhere but you ain't gonna never find him if you keep yourself locked down in your negative thinking attitude," she said. Her mother looked at her and ran her hand through her hair.

"Maybe we both can go out and meet someone, it's been a long time since I been with a man too. How about it?" her mother asked.

Betsy shook her head, "Okay mama," she said. Betsy went into her room and lied down on her bed and looked up at the ceiling and began fantasized about me. She could see herself and me with her four kids playing at a gazebo in the backyard of a huge colonial house we owned. All of her financial worries were over and she was happy and deep in love with me. She knew I was a rare find for any black woman in this day and time. Her mother called, "Betsy baby."

She got up and into the living room and her mother looked at her. It was Friday morning and Betsy was dusting the living room of my house and Gina was sitting at the dining room table. "Miss Gina, how it come by that you and Mr. Henry got together?" she asked.

Gina hesitated for a moment and thought and in a sincere way begin to speak. "Well, Henry and I met a few years ago and he told me of his past failed relationships with black women. He really intended to be with a black female but he could not find one on his economical or social status. He knew he was getting older and he wanted to have kids. I have loved black men all my life because white men just don't have what it takes. They are just not as manly or sexy as a black man. Most of them are just too kinky for me and alot of them are closet bisexuals or like penetration with toys in role reversal relationships and I just can't deal with that."

Miss Betsy looked and was perplexed because she thought

the reason why Henry and Gina were together was because of a weird sexual quirk they both shared. "You mean to tell me you and Mr. Henry are not, excuse but I don't mean no harm, not freaky in some kind of way?" Betsy asked.

"No more than any other couple but of course we do try knew things to add a little spice but we are both straight lovers," Gina said.

Betsy begins to think and was happy and was thinking of some way to get closer to Henry.

"He also told me that a lot of black women past him up were because they considered him a nerd or a sucker and only wanted him for his money. I never really got into it that much but I know there are a lot of problems in your race of people due to your past," Gina said.

"I know I sure would have like to have had him when I was coming along. The men I meet ain't about nothing but a beer can up to their mouth," Betsy said.

"No one recognized he was something special until I came along," Gina said.

"You never know Miss Gina," Betsy said, smiling and dusting.

"So what are you doing for yourself?" Gina asked.

Betsy stopped and turned around. "I don't have much going on right now but me and my mama is going out to a club this weekend and find someone to tickle my blossom. Make me smile deep inside," she said.

Gina smiled. "That sounds like fun where are you going?" she asked.

"It's this little place on the south side where they play blues and alot of handsome, strong, hardworking men go there with their nice, shiny new long cars and they buy the ladies drinks and dance and laugh," Betsy says and starts dancing with her duster.

"Mind if I go out with you?" Gina asked.

"Miss Gina, you will be the only white woman in there and ain't too many black women gonna like to see you in there flirting with black men," Betsy said.

"But I still want to go," Gina said.

"Okay, Miss Gina," she said.

"You don't have to continuously call me Miss Gina all the time, just call me Gina," Gina said.

Later that night Betsy was at home on the phone with her cousin Ida May. "Ida, I work at this black dude house and he married to a white woman and he is very nice looking man," Betsy says.

"You know all these black men who are doing okay is married to white girls," Ida said.

"Look like it but she wants to go out with me and my mama this weekend to look at black men with her tongue hanging out but she just don't know. The first time she even touches one I got something on her to tell her husband," Betsy said.

"She don't have no business with a rich brother anyway, the way all of us black women are hurting now days struggling with kids and no man at home," Ida said.

"Girl, I'm thinking of away to get him for myself. I saw him walk out of the shower naked and boy, does he have something down there," Betsy said.

"It just gonna take a little time honey, that's all," said Ida.

"Shoot, I'm gonna get me one of those nice looking mens tomorrow when we go out even if I have to pay him," Betsy said. Ida laughs. "Yea, girl she just don't know and the man wants kids, I got four," Betsy said.

"You done had your fun and all you need now is a man, a good man," Ida said.

"I am a real good woman," Betsy said.

"Can I go with yall Tomorrow night?" Ida asked.

"Yep, sure can so we can laugh at this white girl," Betsy

says and laughs.

"I remember how you was in high school, a girl could not keep a man because of you and I bet you act so innocent when you over their house working," Ida said.

"Girl, you ought to hear me, it make me sick just to think about it. Yes, Miss Gina this, yes, Miss Gina that and sounding like a whipped slave," Betsy said.

"They probably think you so stupid acting like that huh?" Ida asked.

"Probably so but I don't care I got kids to feed," Betsy said.

"What will you do if she leaves out with another man?" Ida asked.

"I got her right where I want her then," Betsy said.

"I got to go right now but I will call you tomorrow before I come over," Ida said.

"Okay, bye" says Betsy and hangs up the telephone.

CHAPTER THREE--Pressure Mounting

Saturday night had come and Gina drives up Miss Betsy's driveway. Miss Betsy walked over to the window and gazed out as the lights illuminated the living room.

"Who is it baby?" Mama asked.

Miss Betsy smiling, "it's Miss Gina, the little white girl I work for."

She opens the door as Gina walks up to the door. "Hey, Betsy," she said. She enters and looks around and sees the handmade quilts that were covering the couch. "These are so pretty I always wanted to know how to do this," Gina said.

"You must be Gina," said mama.

"That's me, you are Miss Betsy's mama," Gina said.

"Yep," mama said.

"Mama, it's 8:00' clock," Betsy said.

"Gina, I know you just came here but those men are pouring into the club right now and I'm ready to go," Mama said.

"Are you ready to go?" asked Gina.

"Yea, let's get out of here and meet the public," Mama said.

"Let's go in my car," Gina said.

Later in the club they were seated near the door to watch the men arrive. One man entered, he was tall, wore a gold chain around his neck and had a diamond studded watch. "That man sure looks nice," Betsy said.

"I like the gold," Mama said.

"I like his wide chest, I wonder if it's hairy. I just love men with a hairy chest," Gina said.

"Girl, you better watch yourself. You know you're married and Mr. Cook don't take no mess," said Mama.

They all laugh when this one light complexion black male

enters and they stop and all their eyes are affixed to his handsomeness and quiet, mysterious mannerism. He passes by them and waves. "Damn, Mama he is so fine," Betsy said.

"Boy, if I were only fifteen years younger," Mama said.

Gina just looks at the guy smiling. The waiter comes over and asks, "what will you lovely ladies have tonight?"

"Lets all get Margarita's, okay?" Mama asks.

Everyone nods their head in agreement. The music just begins to play. An older gentleman comes up and takes Mama to the dance floor; they dance for two songs while Betsy and Gina are sitting at the table talking. From across the room the handsome quiet guy is looking at them smiling when finally their eyes make contact with his and he walks over to the table. "May I join you?" he said.

"Sure," Betsy said.

"My name is Michael and you?" he asked.

"I am Betsy and this is Gina," Betsy said.

"Nice to meet you. I see you girls are alone tonight," Michael asked.

"It's been along time since I been out," she says as she put her hand on his thigh and begins to caress it.

"I see," said Michael.

"Are you married?" Betsy asked.

"No, I am single," said Michael.

"So am I. Do you ever think about getting married?" Betsy asked.

"No, I haven't met the right girl yet," Michael said.

"Oh," said Betsy.

"Hey Gina, would you like to dance?" Michael asked.

"Why not," Gina said. They go to the dance floor and start dancing.

"I wonder why all good-looking black men like white girls?" Betsy asked herself as she sits alone.

She watches Michael dance as he is a good dancer and has

an excellent body. "I sure would like to go home with him tonight," Betsy said.

"I love the way you dance," said Gina.

"I just want to get close to you.   I've been watching you since I got in this place," Michael said.

"Let's go sit down; I am a little tired and its hot in here," Gina said

They walk back to the table and Betsy looks at Michael. "Would you like to dance?" she asked.

"Let's go," said Michael. Gina sits at the table and drinks her drink, then she orders another and another as Betsy and her mother dance the night away.

Mama is talking to the club photographer. "When my daughter," she points at Betsy, "comes off the dance floor I want you to come over to our table and take a picture," Mama said then returns to the table. She looks at Gina and asks, "are you enjoying yourself honey?"

"I am just looking around drinking," Gina said as she is noticeably drunk.

Michael and Betsy return to the table. Michael sits next to Gina and the photographer comes up to them. "Ya'll ready?" he asks.

Everybody strikes a pose and Michael places his arm around Gina and the lights flash. "That was a nice picture," photographer said. The older gentleman returns and Mama gets up and goes with him, "I will see ya'll sometime tomorrow, I am going with him," she said.

She meets the photographer at the door and gets the pictures and they depart.

"I don't think tonight is my lucky night," Betsy said.

"There's plenty of guys in here," Michael said.

Betsy is sad as she had her sights set on him. "Are you ready to go?" asked Gina.

"Yea, let's get out of this place," Betsy said.

"Can I get your phone number?" Michael asked Gina.

"No, I don't think that would be a good idea," she said.

"Oh, I get it, ya'll a little on the funny side," Michael asked.

"No, not that either," Gina said.

"Well, we will be seeing you," Betsy said.

I watch TV all night wondering where Gina was. The doorbell rang and I sprang up to answer. Gina was at the door drunk. "Are you Okay?" I asked. With that I lifted her up in my arms and took her to the bedroom. I then laid her gently on the bed and gazed at her lovingly and caressed her forehead. "Never a day has past that you have not filled my life with joy and contentment. You have freed my heart of the heavy burden of loneliness, personal isolation and replaced it with warmth and understanding. Freed me of the emotional prison that had my spirit and soul jailed for all eternity. Caring and love is your gift to me and I thank the day you came into my life, Gina."

She looked up at me smiling. Vividly the day lingers in my mind every day for the rest of my life new as a morning dew that will run as a river to the sea and to the ocean to give drink to all of the earth and bring prosperity to their crops and bear fruit on all the trees. Surely it was God who sent this angel to me. I took off my clothes and laid next to Gina in bed holding her close to me as I went to sleep.

Noon the next day. Gina was walking around with a hangover from last night as Miss Betsy was moving about cleaning. "That sure was a nice looking fellow that was liking you last night," Betsy said.

"You know I'm married and I love Henry," Gina said.

"But if you wanted to you could have had that man, girl," Betsy said.

"Your Mama sure did have a good time," Gina explained.

Miss Betsy laughs, "that's how Mama always been even

with paw paw she was the same way. They used to dance with each other in the living room when I was a kid and we used to dance right along with them," she said.

"I was shy when I was younger and liked boys but was too afraid to tell them," Gina said.

"I ain't never been afraid of no man," Betsy said.

Gina walks over to the refrigerator and pours herself a glass of tomato juice. "My head is thumping," Gina said.

"I guess nobody wants me Miss Gina. Didn't a single man approach over my way for me," Betsy said depressed.

"There is somebody for everybody Miss Betsy and do you believe that?" Gina said and looked directly at Miss Betsy.

Betsy shook her head, "I guess you're right," she said as she swept the floor.

At the same time I was at Arnolds' house with Ralph. "Gina was out all night," I said.

"You know I told you about those white girls," said Arnold.

"Hey, hey, my wife is white too," said Ralph.

"Well," Arnold says and stops.

"Oh, she wasn't messing around; she was helping our maid look for a man. She looks so sad all the time and we thought maybe if she had a man in her life it would lift up her spirits," I said.

"Man; you gonna fall for that? That's just a cover," said Arnold.

"Are you crazy?" Ralph asks Arnold. "Every white girl that's with a black man isn't a slut or a whore. What's wrong with you?" he asked.

"You see Arnold's got one of those sisters' whose just waiting for him to get his doctors' degree, start practicing medicine and make big money; then she's going to burn him," I said.

"Yea, she's probably scheming with one of her homegirls

right now on how she going to get paid and probably got a man on the side," Ralph said; and we laugh.

"Shirley is a good girl," Arnold said.

"Until she gets pregnant with your baby but don't want you except for child support so she can mess around with a lot of men and have her fun at your expense," I said.

"Man, you know how ignorant these lazy black women are," Ralph said.

"That's you guys point of view," Arnold said.

"It's the truth man," I said.

"They are scum," Ralph added.

"You guys are messed up when it comes to women, you know that," Arnold said.

"Hey man, don't you know that's why black society is deteriorating. It's because of these black women trying to raise our little black boys by themselves. The only thing a woman can do to a young male child is make him a soft, weak, undisciplined loser, who resorts to violence when the world tells him no," I said.

"My mom raised me by herself," Arnold said.

"Your mom got married again when you was ten," Ralph said.

"That man put some discipline in your life didn't he?" I asked.

Arnold said, "yes," hesitantly.

"And that's why you are close to becoming a doctor right now instead of a felon. Women can have a detrimental effect on a male psyche in the developing years. You know that, you taken psychology," I said.

"I don't believe in psychology I just took it because I had to," Arnold said.

"I think we got him on the defensive," Ralph said.

"We'll let up off him for now, but we will get him again," I said.

"You know these teenage boys now days are so violent and they sell drugs and pack guns and kill people. I am talking about boys as young as ten years old. When I was growing up, we had an extended family with our neighbors and teachers. Professional athletes use to come and spend time with us and we believed we could grow up and be somebody."

"These athletes now days don't care about anybody except themselves and being seen on TV with an audience full of little white kids," Ralph said.

"I grew up in an extended family. I used to play catch with Bob Hayes number 22 before Emmitt Smith had it for the Dallas Cowboys. He was the worlds fastest human and won the hundred-yard dash in the 1960 Olympics," I said.

"Our teachers were mean too. I remember Miss "Razor Strap"Tyne . . . I spent more time bending over for a spanking than standing up or sitting down in her class. I was too afraid not to do my work in her class," Ralph said.

"You see, you guys can remember the good things our race has to offer," Arnold said.

"Here he goes again," I said.

"We promised to give him a break," Ralph said.

"I got to go home it's about 3 o'clock," I said as I looked at my watch. Later as I was walking down the street, I saw some little girls playing music and dancing. As I was passing by and one of the little girls came up to me and grabbed my hand. She lead me over to where they were at and starting dancing with me. I begin to dance and the little girls started laughing at me. "I have to go," I told the girls as I smiled.

The little girl that I was dancing with told the others that I was her boyfriend. "I don't think your mother would approve of that," I said.

"My mother don't have to know," she said. I laughed, waved goodby and departed.

8pm later at Miss Betsy's place.

    They are sitting down at the table discussing about the night before. "Mama you got the picture?" Betsy asked.

"Yep, right here," she said.

Betsy looks at it and smiles, "look at that white girl all wrapped up with Michael. She just don't know the trouble she would be in if Mr. cook saw this," Betsy said.

"Ida didn't even show up," Mama said.

"I am going to give her a call later. She probably couldn't get away from her old man you know how jealous he is," Betsy said.

"I sure enjoyed myself girl," said Mama.

"Mama quit it," Betsy said and walked over to the telephone. "I think I am going to call Ida right now and see what happened to her."

"Hello Ida, this is Betsy."

"Oh, hey girl. How did it go last night?" Ida asked.

"It went fine. We got a picture of that white girl all hugged up with this really handsome brother. He didn't want me but I tried to get him," Betsy said.

"My old man put his foot down and wouldn't let me leave the house. He was getting ready to kick my butt," Ida said.

"I think the next thing I will do to this white girl, is write down Michael's telephone number on a piece of paper and leave it where Mr. Cook will find it," Betsy said.

"That's a good idea. Don't no white girl deserve a black man like him anyway," Ida said.

"Then I think I will plant the picture somewhere else where he can find it a week later and write some sweet lines on the back," Betsy said.

"Girl, you are something else," Ida said.

"But I think before all that I will start calling their house;

when I know that Mr. Cook is there from a pay phone and hang up when he answers," Betsy said.

"You are diabolical," Ida said.

"Last but not least I will keep that white girl going out with me to further arouse suspicion and distrust," Betsy said.

"Divide and conquer," Ida said.

Betsy laughs, "Yep, and any other thing I can do to break them up in my own sneaky way. I will be making my move on Mr. Cook but not directly, maybe get him to have sex with me and that will further encourage the break up as I have a well-planned slip of the lip," Betsy said.

"You ain't no good," Ida said.

"I am tired of walking around saying, "yes, sir or no ma'am" stuff. I am going to get that man for myself or break it up so nobody can have it," Betsy said angrily.

"Here comes my old man, I don't want him to think I am talking to a man so I am going to let you go, you be careful and don't get caught. . . bye," Ida said.

"Bye," said Betsy and hung up the phone. At the same time Gina is on the phone talking to her sister Lisa. "You mean to tell me you went out with your maid to a club?" Lisa asked.

"Yea, we had a good time and this very nice looking black guy came over to me and could not keep his hands off of me," Gina said.

"What did Henry say about you being out all night?" Lisa asked.

"He trusts me. He didn't say anything," Gina said.

"Are you guys sex life going strong or is it getting cold?" Lisa asked.

"Everything is lovely between us and we are trying to have a baby," Gina said.

"You told me that the last time I talked to you which was when . . . four months ago?" Lisa said.

"I know," Gina said.

"I wouldn't trust that maid if I were you because some of these black girls see a white girl with a black man and they become real jealous and you especially don't want to be doing any flirting with strange men when she is with you because it's going to come right back in your house," Lisa said.

"She is a very respectful woman Lisa, with four kids. She would never do anything like that," Gina said.

"Live and learn girl, live and learn. You can never trust a woman, except me because I don't date black men. I think they are all ugly and look like monkeys. That dark skin and those big lips, all they have to do is swing on a vine," Lisa said.

"I don't like it when you talk that way," Gina said.

"Mother didn't say anything when you married Henry, but you know what? She really didn't like it but she didn't want to hurt your feelings. I speak my mind whether you like it or not but I love you," Lisa said.

"I love you, too," Gina said.

"Well, baby girl . . . I got to go to sleep; I work two jobs. My man don't make the money yours does," Lisa said.

"Okay, will talk to you later, bye" says Gina and hangs up the phone.

I went into the living room and sat beside Gina. I look at her and begin to tickle her here and there; she asks me to stop but I continued and next we are on the floor wrestling playfully and laughing. When she finally gives up, I look at her and asked her if she remember the poem I read to her last night.

"No, what poem?" she asked.

"I can't remember because I made it up as I looked down at you. I love you," Gina. I gave her a deep, long, soulful kiss.

"The sea was roaring but love withstands, I

wrote your name in the sand and it lived longer
than most sand castles and crustacean homes and
let alone the true love between two."

"The art of love is drawn from the heart with
well-sculptured words crafted with passion and molded with
lust, caresses of gentleness and laid to bear the soul and leave
it naked in the wake of a climax"
"Is there any rock unturned, is the book not read
completely and such as in love where two lovers explore the
boundaries of their sexuality and finding many new desires
uncover by trial and convicted by their lust?"

CHAPTER FOUR--Suspicious Minds

Four days later, I was looking through my drawings when I came upon this picture of Gina with a young black male in her arms with Betsy seated in a night club.

I wondered for a moment but dismissed any thoughts of her playing around on me. Later that afternoon Betsy came into the bedroom and was vacuuming the carpet. "How you Mr. Cook," she said.

"I am fine Betsy," I said as I lied in the bed in my pajamas.

"You look real relaxed but on natures edge and ready," she said.

"What does that mean?" I asked.

"Well, it means that you look like you are ready to get a hump in your back and make an ugly face from intense pleasure," she said.

I laughed, "oh, sexually ready?" I asked.

"Yea sir, that's what I meant but I wanted to be ladylike when I was talking," she said.

"Betsy, you are always ladylike," I said.

"Is that good, Mr. Cook?" she asked.

"Yea, it shows you have class," I said.

She blushed, and giggled.

"Nobody ever told you that?" I asked.

"Not in a long while," she said.

"Why haven't you found another man? How long has it been since you dated someone?" I asked.

She turns the vacuum off. "It's been a long while and I am all backed up and due for a good lay," she said.

"Well, good luck," I said.

Betsy left my bedroom and returned to her room and sat for a while trying to find a way to get closer to me. She looked out of the window. It was a clear day and she saw birds in the trees and squirrels climbing up and down the tree chasing each other and playing games. She begins taking off her clothes and she screamed like she was deep distress and I ran to her room. "What's wrong?" I asked with deep concern and she held me without a bra in her panties.

"It's a mouse and he just ran in that closet," she said.

"We don't have any mice or rats in this house," I said.

Her body begins to relax on mine and she begins to breathe real hard. "Please take me, Mr. Cook, right here, right now, please," she begged.

"Betsy, put your clothes on and stop this. I don't want to have sex with you," I said.

"Please don't tell Miss Gina," she said.

"I won't; just don't do this again," I said.

"I could not help myself, you are so fine Mr. Cook," she said.

I looked at her sympathetically and left. Betsy sat there on the bed with her head down in shame. I started to think that couldn't I have just given her an orgasm to raise her moral but what would be the outcome if she gets emotionally attached. Later on that night Gina returned home after shopping with her sister Lisa. "Did you get me anything?" I playfully asked.

She looked in her bag, "let me see here," she said.

"If it takes that long then I know the answer," I said.

"I got you a key chain," she said.

"Oh, it's a little bible. I like that," I said.

"The rest of the stuff I bought from a thrift store," she said and tossed the bag in the kitchen corner.

The phone rings. "I got it," I said. I picked up the phone and said, "hello." The only thing I could hear on the other end was some heavy breathing that intensified; then a sigh of relief, if though someone had just gotten an orgasm and then they hung up. I held the phone for a short while in disbelief as to what had just happened; trying to piece it all together as it did not make sense to me.

"What's wrong?" Gina asked.

"I'm not sure what just happened," I said.

"Well, it had to be something," she said.

"It was someone on the other end and it sounded like a man masturbating over the phone breathing very heavy," I said.

"Let's star 69 the call and see what happens," she said.

I pick up the receiver of the phone and dial star 69. The operator said, "we are unable to give that information due to it was originated on a pay phone."

Betsy and Ida laugh as they hang up the pay phone. "Girl, you sound just like a man," Betsy said.

"We gonna call back again around one o'clock tonight," Ida said.

"I tried to get him to screw me so bad today. I pulled off my clothes, I screamed and when he came in the room I grabbed and said, I saw a mouse," Betsy said.

"No, you didn't," Ida said.

"He wouldn't touch me for nothing. He's so in love with that white girl," Betsy said.

"You just keep working on him and he'll give in," Ida said.

"After we call back again to further confusion, I am going to plant Michael's phone number tomorrow," Betsy said.

"You gonna keep up the pressure, huh?" Ida asked.

"Until I win him," Betsy said.

"What if he never comes around?" Ida asked.

"He will, I haven't found a man yet that I can't work on and have for myself," Betsy said.

1:00 A.M.

Gina and I are in bed when the phone rings. "I wonder who is this calling at this time of night?"

"Hello," I said and the man voice begins to utter dirty sexual words that were not very legible and I hung up mad.

"What's wrong?" Gina asked.

"It's that same prank-caller again," I said.

"Maybe it's Arnold or Ralph playing a joke," she said.

"You don't know anybody who would do that do you?" I asked.

"No," she said.

I looked at her for a moment and a slight suspicion begins to grow inside of me.

9:00 A.M.

The same morning. Miss Betsy is serving breakfast and we are sitting at the table. "Betsy, you wouldn't know anyone who would be calling here late at night would you?" I asked.

"No sir, Mr. Cook, I would never disrespect your house like that," she said.

I looked at Gina and she was still half asleep and I touched her on the leg. "You still look sleepy, did you have something heavy on your mind last night. You tossed and turned all night," I said.

"It must have been something I ate," Gina said.

"You were mumbling and talking also but I couldn't make out who or what it was," I said.

"I was probably calling for a doctor," she said.

"Really," I said.

"Well, what else could it have been? I don't remember anyone moving me that emotionally that I would go to sleep thinking about it," she said.

"Ah, drink your coffee and shut up," I said. She looked at

me and sipped sheepishly. "Daddy runs this house, don't I?"
I asked.

Gina shook her head in agreement.

"Betsy, you can go home right after you finish washing dishes," I said.

"Yes sir, Mr. Cook," she said.

"I am still going to pay you for today," I said.

Betsy smiled.

I opened up my wallet and gave her fifty dollars. "That should help out your household some, don't you think?" I asked.

"Oh, yes sir," she said.

"Matter of fact you can just go right and leave everything, it will be here tomorrow," I said.

She left hurriedly without saying a word. I went into the bedroom and began to get dressed and Gina came in.

"You can go back to bed," I said.

I went to work and decided to leave early. I went to a bar close to the job and met a young pretty white girl named Penny as I slowly drank my beer. "My man left me and I just can't get him off my mind," Penny said.

"Hey, let's play some music, okay?" I said. I went up the jukebox and started looking through the selections; I picked out some Billy Joel and I begin to dance as I returned to where I was sitting.

"Oh, you are a dancer?" Penny asked.

"I do a little bit of something sometimes," I said.

"I didn't have any idea he was going to leave me," she said.

"You keep thinking about him and it's going to make you more miserable and you will end up needing a shrink to straighten you out," I said.

"I know but he was everything I wanted in a man," she said.

"You know what? Every time a woman loves that strongly, a man always hurt them," I said.

"I know he cared about me," she said.

"He may have cared but he did not love you, that's why you are alone sitting here with me," I said.

"I gave him my all, the very best I had," she said.

I finished my drink for I was tired of listening to her and I looked at her and she looked so depressed and hurt. I knew there was nothing I could say or do that would make her feel better. Inside of me I was hoping I would never be hurt like her. I had been hurt in the past but I know I would never let it happen again. "I got to go. It was nice meeting you," I said.

She didn't even acknowledge me because she was so deep into her hurting state. I left and got into my car and went home. At the same time Betsy was talking to her cousin Ida on the phone. "I got him wondering now about her whether she truly loved him or not. I could tell by the way he treated her this morning at breakfast," Betsy said.

"What happened?" Ida asked.

"He was wondering about that phone call we made last night," Betsy said and they laughed. "Just wait till he finds those phone numbers I planted this morning," Betsy continued.

"You do all the work; what does he need her for anyway?" Ida said.

"I know all I got to do is just start having sex with him and I am his complete woman," Betsy said.

"I hear you girl," Ida said.

4:00 P.M. later.

I drove up the drive way and Gina was outside as usual watering her roses. I walked by her without saying a word. I pulled off my coat and threw it on the couch and went to the refrigerator and open up a can of pop. I went to the window and gazed outside for a while. I went into the bedroom and took off my wedding ring; then I found a piece of paper with a man named Michael written on it with his phone number and best time to call. I looked at it and began to think about all the strange occurrences, the phone calls and I put it in my pocket. I returned to the living room and turned on the television to listen to the news. Gina came inside and looked at me and I looked at her eye to eye without expression. "What's wrong, you didn't even speak to me?" Gina said.

"Sit down over there in that chair," I said. I reached into my pocket and brought out the photo I found. "I have a few artifacts for you to explain," I said, as I handed her the picture.

She looked at it. "Oh, that's Michael, I met him when I went out with Betsy last week," she said.

"What about this?" I asked and handed her his phone number.

"I didn't get his phone number and neither did I do anything with him," she said.

"What about those phone calls late at night that we have been getting?" I asked.

"I don't know who that is and I didn't get his phone number. I don't know how this got here," she said.

"I don't know what to believe," I said.

"Maybe Betsy got his number; she does use our phone sometimes to call up different people," she said.

"We asked her that this morning," I snapped.

"I don't know," she said.

"I trusted you. I didn't even ask one question about what you did that night knowing that you wouldn't mess around with anyone," I said.

"I didn't do anything," she said. Gina got up and tried to sit next to me and console me but I was very angry.

"Don't touch me and get back over there in that chair," I

shouted.

She begins to cry. "Now the crying game, huh? You know I am not going to fall for that," I said.

I stood up and looked at her.

"Shut up right now, damn it," I shouted.

She fell to her knees and cried on my shoes and kissed them. I was totally unfeeling or merciful by this time. I pushed her away and started to slap her but refrained myself. "I am going to whip your butt with my wide belt and Betsy too for trying to get me to screw her this morning," I said.

"Betsy tried to what?" Gina asked. She was visibly angry.

"Just shut up and be ready for your punishment tomorrow to prove your obedience to me. You can tell Betsy, if she don't want to submit she can just not come back," I said. I got my coat and drove over Arnolds' house.

Gina called her sister on the phone. "Hello, baby sister," Lisa said.

"He thinks I was seeing another man," Gina cried.

"I told you about making friends with that damn niger maid," Lisa said.

"She tried to have sex with him behind my back and now he is going to whip both of us with his wide belt," she cried.

"Maybe you deserve a spanking. I love you," Lisa said.

"I didn't do anything," Gina cried.

"Is he going to fire that niger?" Lisa asked.

"If she doesn't take the whipping," Gina cried.

"You can always come over my place until things boil over," Lisa said.

"I am going to surrender to him and take it," Gina cried.

"Well, that's up to you but if you need anything or change your mind, I'm here for you," Lisa said.

"Okay, thanks," Gina sniffles.

I was sitting around with Arnold talking about what had just happened. He looked at me sympathetically. "You know

I don't believe in interracial stuff anyway but you are my friend and I am not going to tell you anything negative," Arnold said.

"I would like to ask you if I can stay here with you until I work things out with her," I said.

"Yea, that's Ok," he said.

"I am going to go back over and get some clothes tomorrow," I said.

"I am kind of tired so I think I am going to go to sleep," Arnold said as he walked into his bedroom.

I tried to go to sleep but found it very difficult for I was extremely upset. My jaws were shut tight and I grounded my teeth thinking about what I was going to do to Gina and Betsy in the morning. I knew in all likelihood that Gina hadn't done anything but I knew also that with my easygoing nature that it leaves me vulnerable to such infidelities so I must take decisive, harsh counter measures for Gina to think about in the future. Her bottom will be very sore and tears of redemption in her beautiful hazel eyes. I know that she is a good girl but I must execute discipline and reestablished my position of strength and dominance in our relationship. In Betsy's case, what I am doing is an act of kindness for I could just fire her and she is out in the street to struggle and compete in a hard, cold world with alot of other women who lack the job skills to get a decent paying job, but also there is a backlash to taking this mode of operations with her. She could more probably file a civil lawsuit and jail time for me but I believe her infatuation with me enthralls her need to please and honor my peaceful resolution and yet another woman kneeling before me to receive correction of lewd and unacceptable behavior. Who would ever think upon first glance that this peaceful, sedate lady would bare her body in passionate lust and risk her source of income? It just goes to show the mental instability and growing sleaziness of our decaying society and low morality of some mother figure black women. Where has decency gone and how will it be restored? I ponder these thoughts in great concern and yet unabashed in outer expression. I finally went to sleep. I kept dreaming seeing myself in scenarios where I was dodging a tornado in broad daylight and hiding behind a strong built structure with huge rocks cut into place like sphinx and barely getting out of the way. I awaked in a cold sweat wondering if there is some of type retribution in the fate that I decided for Gina and Betsy.

7:00 A.M.

I was at my door turning the key. The sun had not risen yet and the birds had just started to sing, I took this as the making of what would be a beautiful day. When I entered through the door, Gina ran up to me with watery eyes with her head down in sorrow. She grabbed me by the hand and said, "let's get this over with," as we went into the bedroom. The belt was already on the bed and Gina lowered her panties and bent over the bed.

"Where is Betsy?" I asked as I picked up the belt.

"She's in her room," she said.

"Did you tell her what she had coming or leave?"

"Yes," she said, very humbly.

"So, what did she decide?"

"She will accept the punishment," she said.

"You have twenty lashes coming my love and I hope you learn a lesson from this," I said, as I raised the belt gazing at her beautiful, smooth white buttocks and I proceeded to really lay into her hard and she wept and begged for forgiveness with every stroke. Betsy heard the commotion and came in to investigate as I just gave Gina her last stroke. Gina fell to her knees in front of me, "I'm sorry," she cried.

"Get up and go wash up," I snapped.

I looked at Betsy and said, "you're next."

She looked at me as she wearing black spandex tights. She began slowly to pull them down, "you don't have to take them off just bend over this bed," I said. Without saying a word she kneeled over with her buttocks out in a most vulnerable position. "Betsy, I am ashamed of you coming onto me. I ought to fire you but I love you too much to see you out in the cold," I said.

She looked back at me as I continued. "I am going to give you five strokes." I didn't whip Betsy as hard as my wife and I could sense the sensuousness she was deriving after the third stroke. Her sides clasped not in pain but in an orgasmic way as she moaned loud and I stopped. "Betsy, get out of here," I snapped. Betsy returned to her room and was very wet in her spandex. She rubbed her bottom and reminisced what had just happened as she pulled down her tights and lay on the bed bare, still feeling the stinging sensation of the belt. She began to work her lust vigorously with passion. I had my bags packed and as I walked out the door, I heard the sound of a female having a loud, intense climax from Betsy's window. I didn't know what to think. I got in my car and drove around for a while trying to get a perspective on everything that had happened up to this point in my life. I had no answers for anything but I knew time and patience would provide them later.

CHAPTER FIVE--Male Bonding

Later that afternoon I was sitting with Arnold in the kitchen and we conversed casually as he was writing an essay. "When will you start your practice?" I asked.

"Hopefully very soon," he said.

"Don't start assisting suicide," I said.

He dropped his pen and stared at me for a second then said, "that's a very serious matter." He paused then continued, "alot of those people who know they're going to die and there's no known cure, they are in so much pain and misery."

I didn't say anything for a moment because I was feeling very foolish.

We then heard someone knocking at the door. "That must be Mr. Knox," he said, as he went to open the door.

He and Mr. Knox entered the kitchen. Mr. Knox was carrying a case of beer. "Hey Henry," he said.

"How are you, Sir?" I replied.

"It's going to be a beautiful day of intelligent black brothers socializing," he said.

Arnold began to gather his scattered papers.

"Boy, what the heck are you doing?" Mr. Knox said to Arnold, "and they tell me you left that hazel-eyed girl," he said to me.

"For a little while," I said.

He looked at me and popped open a can of beer and sat down. "Boy, let me tell you the story of old Ramos." Mr. Knox leaned back in his chair and relaxed. As pulled out a cigarette he began to speak. "I knew a guy named Ramos, a few years ago; he was black. The thing about Ramos was he was getting older; he was a very decent, good man. He'd give you the shirt off his back. He ended up marrying this young black girl, she was an urbanite and would probably end up pregnant by some poor character Negro and he'd leave her. I'm talking about the type of girl she was just to get you to understand where I am coming from."

"We understand what you are saying, Mr. Knox," said, Arnold.

"Well, let me finish then boy," Mr. Knox said and continued. "You see, oh Ramos was highly educated and was a corporate executive back when black people were unheard of getting positions like that; but, any way back to the story, he was good to that girl and she ran around behind his back with every Tom, Dick and Harry that there was. He went to the doctor a year ago because he was feeling tired and weak all the time. Three weeks later the got the results back from the doctor and he told him he had AIDS and the only lover the man had was her."

Arnold looked at me with a sly grin and I got two beers and handed one to Arnold. "Mr. Knox got a lot of stories. He's been around forever," Arnold said and laughed.

"How old are you Mr. Knox, about sixty-five?" I asked.

He hesitated for a while and took a sip of his beer, "I am seven-three and going to turn seventy-four in June," he said.

I turned my beer up and let it go down my throat. The chill of it going down gave me goose bumps all over my body; I belched strongly and Arnold laughed.

"Mr. Knox, I don't think like you and Arnold. To me, it doesn't matter what color you are, its how you live and treat others. Before you can love anyone else, you must have a great love of self and inner peace which is totally untouched by an ever changing world. Most people's attitudes are shaped by their prosperity which influence their behavior and self esteem level. Some people don't have any virtues or values for if we live without them we are no more than animals or savages who try to outsmart and undermine the law of the land, which shape us as civilized people."

Arnold rolls his eyes, and says, "he's on a roll now."

"The poor often are caught up in this trap because they see no way out; but everyone in life has their chance to achieve if they believe they can and persevere. I was poor and my mother worked as a maid in a planter's mansion. Now I'm a senior executive. It was a hard, lonely road but I kept pushing and learned every day from life's mistakes until I fulfilled my dream. A lot of times I was rejected by my own people. Black women wouldn't talk to me and called me a nerd; if they did talk to me they thought they could trick me out of my money because they assumed I didn't have any street sense. This is the type of things intelligent, ambitious black-men encounter and we suffer alot of humiliation and rejection because of jealousy by other black people feeling left behind. We are strangers and foreigners in a culture, the neighborhoods and the land that produced us, if though we have committed crime to seek success."

Mr. Knox just looked at me as he drank his beer. Now he is feeling the effects of the alcohol, "I got a story for you," he said. "Now yall sit back and listen; you'll get another chance to talk, but let me tell you the story of Jackie Joe Johnson. I knew this kid, young white kid, named Jackie Joe Johnson. His fantasy was to rescue a female from a muscular, tall, black man who was making very aggressive and unwanted advances to her. He'd beat the black guy up and then walk away with the girl like he was some kind of big hero. The white boy, the hero type of thing. Jackie was not a big man, he had arms like broom sticks and a chicken neck that bobbed up and down when he walks like a homosexual. A lot of people say he did some time in the pen, serving a black stud who made him wear dresses and sold his body to anybody who wanted him for a cigarette. I think 'ol Jackie wanted to win back his self-respect because he was a sex slave to a black man in jail. A lot of racist white guys are gay or have been feminized by black men. The only reason they hate you is because they can't open up your zipper."

Arnold and I laughed, by then we had drunk four beers while Mr. Knox talked.

"All white men are punks," said Arnold, "and they all have those homosexual tendencies about them, if not early in life, it comes out later. They have sex with animals."

"Shut up," I snapped, "we don't need to hear that, let's just have a good time."

"Oh yea, your wife, I forgot," Arnold said.

"Not that," I said.

Mr. Knox looked at us and rubbed his chin. "This is a gentlemanly conversation between us black men," Mr. Knox said.

"I am going to tell you something about my wife and the black women I have met," I said. "The black woman always tries to get her way and if you don't agree with something that they are saying, they try to say that you have a problem. If you don't get along with your mother, they brand you as a psycho or bad person who needs counseling. I guess all of them think they're perfect and the black man is always wrong. They believe they perfected domestication and black men don't have a clue; but that's just a game to get the ball in their hands so they can fornicate, be deceptive and set you up to steal your money when you give in to it. How many of them didn't get along with their fathers and have already made families looking for a successful, hard working man to take care of the burden she had made by being promiscuous with low morals and walking around like a slut thinking they got to get paid for someone to be with them?" I finished.

Arnold's mouth was open and Mr. Knox looked at me and shook his finger, "you made some good points their boy," he said. "When I was growing, men were men and women were women but now the women want to be men and the men want to be women. Some of them get their hair done in a beauty shop."

"I know," I said and I looked at Arnold, "don't you say nothing just sit there. I almost didn't make it as far as I am today; because when I first started out, I worked at Zales as a computer operator and this young half-black, half-Cajun girl was my supervisor. She chased me every day and I would tell her no again and again because I wasn't into larger women but I am going to tell you she was very pretty and had long black hair. She liked me so much she would go to her desk and just cry. I would pass by her in the hall and see tears in her eyes. I felt sorry for her and it really wore on me to see her so sad. I decided I would give her a chance and time.   I came onto her and told her that I liked her. She went straight to the manager and got me in trouble for sexual harassment. She seemed to be happy after she did it because her eyes were full of life, if though she got off sexually to do that. The manager only wrote me up but I couldn't work with her anymore because I felt bad every time I looked at her. I never knew what her motive was for leading me on and doing that. Black women have never worked out for me; but with Gina, she helps me in every way and not against me and that's the difference between her and black women."

"I have never messed with them," said Mr. Knox. "I like black women, like Arnold; but I do understand what you are saying. That's very sad that no black woman was worthy of you because you are one intelligent brother whose got it together."

Arnold interrupts, "don't tell him that," he said. "His ego will swell . . . largely; and, I do mean large," he said.

Mr. Knox looked at the beer, "yall drink up," he said. With that he pulled out a beer for each one of us and himself. "I got another story for yall," he said, and with that he grinned. Just when he begins to open his mouth there was a knock at the door. Arnold goes for to see who it is. "This must be Ralph," he said, "he's always late."

"I'm going to wait 'till they come back to tell my story," Mr. Knox said.

"Yep," I said. Then Arnold and Ralph came in.

"Late as always," said Mr. Knox, "should we even give him a beer?"

"I already had a few," Ralph said.

"Sit down and let me tell my story," said Mr. Knox, he put his hand to his head for a moment, "yall made me lose my train of thought."

"Let our late comer speak his mind," I said and smiled.

Ralph grabbed a beer and popped the top, "you see these young brothers walking around selling drugs and thinking they look good. I was downtown the other day and one of them walked up to me trying to sell me drugs. I don't know how or why he came up to me; I had on my business suit for work. I guess he thought I was a lonely, stupid nerd and would fall for anything. I acted like I didn't hear him or see him. They wear those baggy pants, belt down to the knees. Man, if I had done that when I was growing up, my mother would have pulled them off and beat me in the frontyard in my underwear."

"They must come from a family with a single mom because I know there is no way I would let a son of mine dress like that," Ralph said.

"They are poor character punks, that's all. Poor character punks who want everything free or easy," I said.

Arnold quickly spoke, "that's not what it is, these young brothers are trying to make it anyway they can because they don't see a future for themselves. They don't respect you or care about you because they feel like you are responsible for it," he finished.

Mr. Knox stood up and spoke with authority, "nothing is

a substitute for education and hard work. They lack faith and faith comes from spirituality.   God is missing in their lives and probably love too," he exclaimed.

"Whose fault is that?" I asked.

No one answered.

"I sure am glad we could get together here today to have our little chat, drink beer and have this good conversation," Mr. Knox said. "I've heard in Dallas, Texas of black-men getting together and drinking beer. Then there's a fight, or someone gets killed, when they get together there; but we are educated black men, those nigers are nigers and we are real men," Mr. Knox said. "We are above that. We are above the rim," he shouted.

We all laughed. After a few hours of talking everyone went to sleep.

I awaked Saturday, the next morning, to the smell of breakfast, eggs and bacon frying. Mr. Knox and Ralph had left. Arnold walked in the living room where I was lying on the couch. "I am going to have to buy a new couch after you finish wearing that one out," he said.

"I hope I won't have to be here too much longer," I said.

"I cooked breakfast so get up broken heart," Arnold said, playfully.

"I don't cook as good as Gina or your Maid but it's kept me alive all this time."

"Thanks, I might divorce Gina and marry you this time around," I said.

"What are we going to do about sex?" Arnold asked.

"We won't have any," I laughed.

"I don't think my girl would go for that anyway," he said.

"I haven't seen her around lately," I said.

"She don't like the idea of a black man being married to a white girl," he said.

"No one does, Arnold not even you," I said.

"But you are my friend," he said.

"This is a free country," I said, "and no one owns me.   I do what I want."

"That's true but at a price," he said.

"Rejection," I said, "but I've been rejected all my life so at least I got one person on my side, my wife."

"Where are you at right now?" he said.

"Here for a little while, only temporary," I said.

"What do you think she is doing right now?" he asked.

"I don't know," I said.

"Do you wonder if she misses you?" he asked, "or is she in someone else arms?"

"I will find out," I said, "you can't hide all the signs and I can always hire a detective if I suspect something. I don't think she is doing anything; she's too clean and honest," I said.

"Your decision and I hope it's the right one," he said.

Later we were sitting at the table and I was sipping coffee, "I think I am going to call Gina today."

"How many days has it been now?" Arnold asked.

"About two weeks and it feels like a year. Do you really know how close we are?" I asked.

Arnold shook his head.

"Very close, she closer to me than my mother," I said.

"I was writing some stuff about politics and I would like to read it to you," he said as he went into the bedroom. My mind was wondering what type of militant stuff I would have to listen to as he shortly returned with papers in his hand and sat down.

"I guess you will want my opinion when you're through," I asked.

"That's what friends are for," he said. "You see we had things good in the Jimmy Carter years. He was a good man," he said, as I looked at him cynically. He continued, "Carter cared about everybody in this country and he was a Christian man. He wanted to see everyone with the ability and determination achieve the American dream. Ronald Reagan was about the unification of the white race through political and legislative avenues to alter our social structure and create a detrimental pathological device to destroy the black man. George Bush wasn't really a bad man and when Clinton beat him I was glad and I wrote this about Bob Dole."

There was a knock at the door. "That must be my girl," he said, as he walked to the door.

He returned shortly with Shirley. She looked at me with contempt and cast her eyes down as she spoke. "Hi Henry," she said, unsuccessfully hiding her bitter feelings about me.

"Hello," I said, and looked at Arnold.

"I'm going to go drive around for a little while. I'll see ya' later," I said, and with that I exit the door. I got into my car and drove around. I came upon a park that I've seen many times before. Today, I noticed the tranquil beauty, the array of flowers, bright colors and the pond with geese swimming unmolested by people, a squirrel very cautiously drinking from it. I parked my car and I had a bag of potato chips and I sat on the grass under a tree. Nearby there was a small patch of dirt where ants were crawling and covering a piece of bread, a trail where they were carrying it away crumb by crumb. I laid back on the grass and looked into the sky. I took a deep breath and I could feel the stress of my problematic life dissipate as my mind wondered into nowhere. Suddenly, I felt a rock hit the bottom of my shoe and I sat up and saw Ralph with a big smile on his face. "I saw your car parked by the curved," he said, and sat down.

"I was just enjoying a little solitude," I said.

"When are you and Gina going to get back together?" he asked.

"Maybe soon," I said.

"We had a wild night last night didn't we?" he asked. I shook my head. "Man, can you imagine what's going on with those two women right now? Boy," said Ralph.

"I don't care and won't until I'm back with them," I said.

"A horny maid and a cheating wife," he laughed.

"I don't think Gina did anything, this is just a game I'm playing to keep her in check," I said. "If you don't take control when challenged it will slowly slip out of your hands then you really got problems," I said.

"My wife knows better," he said.

"You can never be sure. Never say never. Everyone has a point of blind, weak surrender for seduction, no matter how strong or faithful they are," I said.

"That's good point but I know my wife," he said.

I stood up and threw a rock at the geese, "just like I know these geese," I said.

Ralph was sitting drawing lines in the dirt with a stick. "I think we should do something more constructive like going to shoot pool," he said.

"I don't have any money," I said.

"I got you," he said, as he stood up.

I poured out my bag of chips, "feed the birds," I said, as we walked toward our cars. Minutes later, we entered the neighborhood bar and sat down. There wasn't many people inside. The same old bikers were there, the alcoholics, petty hustlers and pool sharks. There was one prostitute who knows better than to approach us and it is rumored she has AIDS. Ralph ordered beer for us as we sat. I looked at him. "Don't you get tired of this place?" I asked.

He stood and tossed four quarters on the counter. "Nope, rack 'em up," he said. I grabbed the quarters and walked over to the pool table. Ralph came over with a que in his hand. "You ever had sex with a black woman?" he asked.

"Well, ah, no," I said. "How about you?" I asked.

"Yea, some are clean, some are dirty and smell but an Asian woman was the best I ever had and I never met a dirty one," he said.

I racked the balls tight and Ralph broke. "Sometimes a black woman cause too many problems in a relationship and I have my career to concentrate on, not a woman causing me problems," he said.

"I've seen your wife; she's beautiful," I said.

He aimed, "see this?" he said, "four ball in the side."

My mind began to go into the past to an occasion when a 14-year-old boy walked up to Ralph and myself. He said, "You brothers think yall all that, but I think yall sound like punks and walk around doing women work."

My eyes were full of rage; I wanted very badly to hit him but I refrained. I said, vehemently, "until you get some education and fill yourself with knowledge, you're just an empty shell walking around reacting passively like a slave. I don't mean to be offensive but that's your mama, your grandmother, all the way back to the day when you were broken in spirit and heart under the whip of slavery and all the way down to you, past generation to generation with plain ignorance and stupidity and rejection of knowledge and the fear of success. Leave me little boy," I said.

CHAPTER SIX--Gina's Revenge

During the same two weeks.

It's 6:30am and Miss Betsy is getting her kids ready for school and cooking breakfast.

In her mind she is wondering what would happen today after she had caused Gina's husband to leave and in another sense she smiled inside of the breakup. She sat down with her mother. "Girl, you ain't said much this morning and I can always know when you got something on your mind," Mama said.

"I am just wondering what's going on with that white lady. Mr. Cook left her," she said.

"That black boy ain't got good sense child, he don't have no business with no white girl. Maybe he is coming around," Mama said.

Miss Betsy looks at the clock. "It's 7:15, it's time for these kids go get out of here to catch the bus. Hey," she shouted, "it's time for yall to catch the bus." The kids ran for the door with their books in their hands and exited. "Yall be careful, you hear?" she shouted, and stood by the door. "I don't know what's going to become of those kids; I'm having such a hard time every day," she said.

"You need a man, kid," said Mama.

"Ain't no man wanting a woman with a house full of kids now a days. They all think they're too good for black women, at least the one's that's worth having," she said.

"Don't give up so easy," said Mama.

"I got to get ready to catch the bus too," she said.

She got her coat and her scarf and buttoned it up. "Mama, I will see you this afternoon," she said, and exited the door. Miss Betsy walked down the street, it was a rather fogged day and a little chilly also with a slight breeze occasionally.

She saw a few kids running to catch the school bus who were a little late. The kids were laughing and one drop her books; but, an older kid picked it up. "These kids now day," she said.

Finally, she made it to the bus stop and sat on the bench. Later on the bus, she was seated next to a handsome man around her age who was wearing work dungaree with a company logo on his shirt. "Good morning," he said.

"Oh . . . morning," she said.

"I had a hard weekend and had to get up early this morning to do what it takes to pay the bills," he said.

"I know that's right," she said.

"What's your name?" he asked.

"Betsy, and you?" she asked.

"My name is Jim. I work at Sears as a refrigerator repairman," he said.

"Is that pretty good money?" she asked.

"Like I said, it pays the bills," he said.

"You married?" she asked.

"My wife and I have been divorced for three years and she is eating me up with child support," he said.

"The man I had, died and I am still grieving his loss, he was a good, good man, it's hard to find a man like him anymore," she said.

"I'm talking to you, but really, I'm through with women. I'm never getting married again," he said.

"Oh, that's too bad because it's alot of good women out here and you are a handsome man," she said.

"Thank you, and you're a pretty nice looking lady yourself," he said.

"You go to church?" she asked.

"I used to when I was a boy but I believe in God," he said.

"Do you drink?" she asked.

"Yea, I do. With all these problems I face, I need a few beers to relax and laugh," he said.

"My husband never touched the stuff," she said, and was thinking inside her mind that this man is not for her. Her stop came up and she rang the bell to get off. "Well, this is my stop," she said.

"Do you have a number that I can call you sometime?" he asked.

"No, I live with my mother, she is kind of sick and I take care of her," she said.

"But what does that have to do with some conversation?" he asked.

"I'll see later, maybe tomorrow," she said, and got off the bus.

Gina heard a knock at the door and went to open it. "It must be that bitch, Betsy," she said. She opened the door and looked at Miss Betsy. "Come in, I got a bone to pick with you," she snapped.

"I know your husband is gone but I am sorry that I cause you problems Gina," she said.

"No, it's Mrs. Gina! Get it? We are no longer on that basis," she barked.

"I knew this wasn't gonna be a good day when I saw the fog," Betsy mumbled.

"My husband is gone because of you! Where did Michael's phone number come from . . . and the picture? Oh, and don't forget the mysterious phone calls late at night." She pointed, "you were naked and called my husband in the room and tried to seduce him, you filthy, nasty, sleazy whore," she screamed.

Betsy dropped her head in shame, and asked, "am I fired?"

"No, my husband didn't want to do that but you are going to work your ass off from now on. No more television and phone calls are limited to three minutes! Get it?" Gina snapped, and grabbed a broom and tossed it to Miss Betsy. "Screw this, it's long enough but it sure is skinny and I know you like em' thick," she barked.

Miss Betsy humbly started sweeping the floor as Gina gave her an angry stare. "I want you to take down every curtain in the house and wash them . . . the small rugs too," she snapped.

"I'm so sorry Miss Gina," Betsy cried.

"Not as sorry as you are going to be. Let me give you twenty lashes with a belt like Henry gave me then," she replied.

Betsy fell to her knees crying.

"No, none of that, get up and push that broom damn it," she barked, "my husband left me and I didn't do a goddamn thing," she continued.

Betsy fought back her emotions, stood up and began sweeping slowly. Gina took the cordless phone and went into the bedroom, slammed the door and called her sister Lisa. "Hello Lisa, this is Gina," she said.

"Hey, baby sister," she said.

"I am putting my foot in Betsy's butt. She came in this morning like she didn't do nothing and then when I started screaming at her, she dropped to the floor in tears. That bullshit is not going to work with me, I am a woman too," Gina said.

"I told you about her; she was after Henry. You can never ever trust a niger bitch like her. She's even more dangerous now than before," Lisa said.

"I am going to break her and make her quit," Gina said.

"Henry won't fire her, huh?" she asked.

"You know how sentimental he is," Gina said.

"That's not one of his best traits, sometimes you got to do what must be done. Have you heard from him?" Lisa asked.

"No, I don't know what he's doing," Gina said.

"Well, I know he loves you. I could tell that a long time ago, he's probably somewhere just cooling off," Lisa said.

"Or maybe he's getting ready to file for divorce," Gina said.

"No hon, I don't think he would do that," Lisa said.

"I guess I'll go back to supervising my little raccoon," Gina said.

"Is that a little racist remark I hear from you?" Lisa asked.

"I can't help it, I am so pissed off at her, I loved that old lady at first and look what she did to me," Gina said.

"We went over this before. You just keep a boss, subordinate relationship with her and everything should be alright but still watch yourself," Lisa said.

"OK sis, I'll talk to you later. Bye," she said, and hung up the phone. Meanwhile, Betsy is taking down curtains in the house and getting them ready to be washed as Gina comes in. "Get on it, I won't that finished today before you go home," Gina said.

"But you only have one washer Miss Gina," Betsy said.

"Then you better manage your time better to get it done . . . I mean it too," Gina snapped.

"I am truly sorry Miss Gina," Betsy said.

"Then you can make it up to me by doing all the things I tell you to do and more and be more obedient for starters," Gina barked.

"I really need this job, Miss Gina, please don't be so cruel to me. I am a human being not a dog," Betsy said.

"How else do you expect me to be after what you did?" she shouted.

"Do you want me to beg on my knees?" Betsy asked.

"No, take twenty lashes across your ass like Henry gave me," she snapped.

Betsy was silent and continued to work at a faster pace.

"You niger bitch," Gina mumbled under her breath and went outside to water her roses. The fog had dissipated and Gina always got a thrill out of her beautiful roses. The sun was shining bright with a supple, occasional breeze, causing her golden locks to give to the wind. Her emotions were lost in confusion; but yet, she still held her dignity. Unsure of her future with the man she loved.

One week later with the abuse continuing, Betsy walked through her door tired and exhausted from yet another day of verbal abuse and drudgery. Her mother looked at her. "Oh child, are you OK?" she said, and helped her to a chair. She shook her head signifying everything was alright. "I am very concerned about you, if things aren't working out I think you should quit," Mama said.

"That's what she wants me to do but I'm going to stick with it," Betsy said. "I got children to feed," she continued.

"She going to work you to death," Mama said. Later that night the phone rang, Betsy picked it up, "hi Ida. What's up?" she asked.

"That what I should be asking you girl," Ida said.

"That white girl is working the hell out of me like I'm her personal slave," Betsy said.

"I'll see if I can find you a job in the kitchen," she said.

"They pay me good but that damn white bitch is on my butt night and day, calling my name like she's dying," Betsy said.

"Her crazy black husband ever called her or come around?" Ida asked.

"I don't think so, at least she ain't said nothing to me about it. I wish he would, then maybe she would stop riding my back all the time," Betsy said.

"Yea," Ida said.

"I sure would like to hit her right in the nose or pour hot grits on her ass while she's drinking some coffee," Betsy said.

"Naw girl," said Ida.

"Yea, I would. I'd burn her little white face and all you will see is two hazel specks through a burnt crust," Betsy said.

"I am going to keep looking around for you for something to do else before you get into trouble," Ida said.

"The last time I beat up a white girl is when I was in high school, I ripped this girl's red hair out by the roots," Betsy said.

"Yea, I remember that, you got expelled for the rest of the year and flunked that grade," Ida said.

"It was worth it," Betsy said.

"You take care; I got to go to sleep," Ida said.

"Ok," said Betsy. Later that night, Betsy laid in bed restless worrying about what she would go through in the morning. Her thoughts were only for the good of her children and her obsession with Henry. Her mind begins to see pictures of him in the nude from when she had seen him after he came out of the shower. She begins to caress herself in her private spot until she fell to sleep. At the Cooks' house Gina is watching television, eating popcorn and drinking a soda until she falls to sleep in a chair in the living room.

8:30am the next day the doorbell rings, Gina gets up from the chair and she had spilled her soda and popcorn all over the floor. She slips in it but doesn't fall and she answers the door. "I know who this is," she said.

Betsy walked inside as the door opened, "Good morning, Miss Gina," she said.

"Get to work. You know what to do," she said.

"Yes, Ma'am, I do at that," Betsy replied.

"Oh, every time I look at you I feel like beating you up, but your eyes are already black like a raccoon," Gina said, and laughed.

Betsy was now putting on her apron and holding back her instinct of aggression; she was unsure how much more she could take.

"Clean up this goddam mess," Gina said, as she pointed at the popcorn and soda on the floor. "I want you to defrost the refrigerator and clean the stove, the fireplace I want you to do last. I want all the ashes removed and put new logs in an orderly fashion. I should not have to tell you this part," Gina said.

"I will get to it, Miss Gina," she said.

"The windows are kind of dirty, so I want those cleaned also and hosed down from the outside. I am going to take a shower and go shopping," Gina said. Gina looked at her with her mouth slightly open in a mocking, contemptuous way.

"You sure you don't want to bend over and take twenty lashes Betsy?" she asked.

But Betsy ignored her and began to move quickly to do her chores. Gina then went into the bathroom. "I ought to kick you ass bitch," Gina yelled, but it was inaudibly to Betsy. All she could hear was an angry voice.

"Will this lady ever forgive me?" she muttered.

A little later on, Gina slipped out of the shower in a bath towel and approached Betsy. "Oh yea, the laundry in the bathroom is filling up, I think you might run a load through and wash my dirty panties," Gina snapped.

Betsy shook her head in silent confirmation.

"Speak to me when I talk to you damn it," Gina barked. "Do you hear me?" she continued.

"Yes, Miss Gina," she said.

Gina went into the bedroom and dressed in a beautiful summer dress with a pair of sandals to match which showed her perfectly pedicured toes and her shapely calves and holding a small black purse. She donned her sunglasses and walked to the door to exit and turned around. "You get hot on these chores and I want to see some progress when I get back here," she snapped. With that, she walked out the door and got into her car and drove away burning rubber in her little red porsche.

Betsy begins to cry but she continued to work and be

strong but actually she was hurt deeper than any emotion could ever show or express. She felt so belittled. Something significant had been taken away from her self worth and reason for life to look to a brighter day but she drudged onward, for she had children to consider and nothing was more important than their well-being even if she has to sacrifice herself to no end. It was the only thing she still had, her motherly instinct to provide for her young.

Gina is in a department store and her eyes are feasting on a nice black velvet skirt. She walks down the aisle and sees a beautiful black and gold paisley evening dress. She smiles and takes it off the rack and looks at it closer and decides to buy it. While in the check out line, Michael catches her eye and she quickly looks away trying not to be seen. He sees her anyway and speaks, "hello, Gina," he said.

"I don't want to talk to you," she said.

He comes closer to her. "Why, you think I am only looking for a one night stand?" he asked.

"I told you; I am married and very happily at that," she said.

"I can't tell," he said.

"I don't appreciate you calling my house late at night," she snapped.

"I don't have your number," he said.

She looked at him if though doubting his word but she sensed that he was sincere and not lying.

"Well, anyway, I don't want to talk to you; my husband is very jealous," she said.

"OK, have it your way, there's other fish in the sea," he said, and walked away.

Now she knew for sure that someone was harassing their household purposely but she knew she could not prove that to her husband. Later she had made her way home and as she walked through the door, Miss Betsy was sweating and working hard and earnestly trying to win back her favor.

Gina looked at her. "Guess who I saw today?" she asked.

"I don't know Ma'am," Betsy said, sheepishly.

"Michael, the guy who we met at the club and he said he didn't call me late at night and I knew he was telling me the truth. I can tell when a man is lying," she said.

"Then who was it then?" Betsy asked.

"Maybe I'm looking at who it is right now as we speak," she said.

"I would never do that to you Miss Gina," she said.

A few days pass and at about 2pm the phone ring. "Get the phone, Betsy," Gina shouted.

Betsy ran through the house to pick up a phone that was easily in Gina's reach. "Hello," Betsy said.

"Hello Betsy, is my wife there?" I asked.

Betsy jumped up in the air in excitement and joy. "It's him, Miss Gina, it's him," she said.

"Who?" Gina said.

"Your husband, Ma'am," she said.

Gina grabbed the phone out of her hands. "Hello," she said.

"Hi Gina, I'm coming home, I hope you learned your lesson, the next time I am gone for keeps," I said.

"I have and I am so glad to hear you," she said, as she begins to cry.

"How yall been getting along?" I asked.

"Everything will be fine when you get back," she said.

"Well, I will be there shortly," I said, and hung up.

Gina hung up the phone.

"I am so glad for you, Miss Gina," she said.

"Nothing has changed for you though," she snapped, and continued crying.

Betsy went back to work singing and humming knowing now she had a mediator who would not tolerate the abuse she has had to take. I was at Arnolds' packing my bags.   "I kind of got use to you being around," Arnold said.

"It was fun, I replied, but I am a married man."

"Let me help you take your bags to the car," Arnold said.

CHAPTER SEVEN--Coming home

It was 7pm and I had stopped by the neighborhood bar to have a few beers. The guy that I had knocked out a few weeks ago was there and looking for trouble again. He was very intoxicated. "Hey, you goddamn asshole," he yelled.

I ignored him and continued to drink my beer. He then threw his beer bottle at me; but it missed miserably. I turned around. "Are you talking to me?" I asked.

"Let's go outside," he screamed.

I got up slowly and headed for the door with him leading the way. Just as he exited, he turned around quickly and sucker punched me. I fell to the floor but I managed to quickly get up. "Oh, is it gonna get dirty and nasty tonight?" I asked. I was in a boxer stance dancing around him. He lunged for me with his head down; I gave him an uppercut that straightened him up. Then I hit him in the stomach and gave him a right cross with all my might and he fell to the floor. "Some people never learn," I said, as I started walking toward my seat.

He managed to get up and he lunged for me again as he let out a loud scream. I turned around just in time to land a blow straight on his chin and he was out for good this time. His girlfriend and a biker carried him out. "I may have to quit this loser, he gets knocked out every time he starts a fight," she said.

The biker kicked him in the buttocks.

"Do you have any lipstick?" he asked.

"Yep," she said.

"Let's have some fun with Tootsie here; we're gonna make him up like a little girl. Tie him to a pallet and let the boys have some fun with him," he said, as they exited the backdoor. A few minutes later they returned and pointed to the other bikers, "Tootsie is tied up and ready to lose her virginity," said the biker.

The bikers rushed outside.

I returned to my seat at the bar and I knew that I would probably never have a problem with that guy anyone after they finished with him. I think he will be ashamed to show his face. My colleagues at work would disclaim me, if they knew that I walked into a place like this anyway. I was going to stay and drink one more but after fighting that guy, it kind of changed my mood to just wanting to go home and watch television.

Later I turned the key through my door and as it opened, Gina ran to me in smiles and tears and embraced me. "I am so glad you're back," she said. I cuffed her cheeks and gave her a deep soulful kiss, lifted her up and carried her to the bedroom. I began to unbutton her shirt, then caressed her buttocks. "I think I kind of like the spanking, as long as it's not too hard," she said.

"If we do it doggie style, I can give you a love slap on your rear now and then," I said.

"I would like that," she said. We both stood up and began to take off the rest of our clothes as fast as we could. She noticed the swelling under my eye where I was cold-cocked by the guy in the bar. "How did that happen?" she asked.

"I had a fight in the bar," I said, as I began kissing her neck.

"Want some ice?" she asked.

"No, I want you now," I said. With that we begin to make love in an ardent animalistic lust with moans, groans, and shouts. The rhythm of our bodies thrashing in hard rapture until we reached a climatic overture and totally sent off our desires and yearnings. We laid perfectly still after what seemed to be an eternity and an outlet of sexual anxieties. I began to caress her back.

"Did you love it dear?" she asked.

"I love making love to you more than any one woman I have ever known," I said. She got up to take a shower. "Bring that body back smelling nice so we can do it again," I said, jokingly. I laid there listening to the water and my mind drifted back to when I was spanking her and my penis got very hard. I looked on the dresser for some Vaseline, thinking that I might want to evade her anally but thought about how I did this one time when I was nineteen and the smell and uncleanness turned me off at the trying this again. If she only knew that she was very closed to taking it up the ass. I got up and went to the bathroom where she was, by this time she had just stepped out of the shower and still dripping with water. I didn't say anything to her but I saw a drop of water slowly running down her back and licked it off slow and sensuously. Then I slapped her on her butt, softly nibbled on her ear lobe, and I began to caress her breasts. Just as I had her in a trance, I stopped abruptly to bring out the feeling of a great tease. She was caught in the middle of sexual need but I stepped into the shower as she looked at me wantonly. "Go to bed and wait for me," I said, and I turned on the water.

She grabbed me by the hand even though I was wet and lead me to the bed and pushed me on it. She got on top and rode me like a cowboy on a wild bull. She worked her woman muscle to achieve her maximum satisfaction like I have never known her to do before. As she reached her orgasm, she dug deep into my flesh but I was absorbed too deeply into the pleasure to feel the pain. She rolled off of me and stood up and lit a cigarette. I went to the bathroom and got a warm towel and returned.

"This is really good sex we are having," she said.

"If you only knew what I was thinking about doing to you while you were in the shower," I said.

"What?" she asked.

"I was trying to find some Vaseline so I could screw you up the ass," I said.

"My body is yours dear," she said.

"I don't want to now but I will keep that in mind," I said.

"I cleaned myself off my private parts with the towel. Where's mine?" Gina asked.

"Nothing separating you from the bathroom and the next time you get in the shower, we are going to do there too," I said.

After a night full of sexual frolic, we went to sleep in each others arms.

8am the next day, Miss Betsy was ringing the doorbell. Gina squinted her eyes and looked out the window.

She got out of bed and opened the door in her underwear. "You know what to do," she snapped.

"Yes Ma'am," Betsy said, and took her belongings to her room. She quickly returned.

"Get with it," Gina said.

"Is he back?" Betsy asked.

"Yea, he is but that don't mean you are going to get a chance to gawk over him," Gina said, sarcastically.

"I'm glad yall back together, Miss Gina," Betsy said.

"Kiss my ass," Gina said, as she walked out of the room.

"Betsy, is that you?" I shouted.

"Yes sir, Mr. Cook, it's me alright," she replied.

"Can you sit down?" I asked, "I didn't do you too bad; when I left I heard you doing yourself," I said.

"Naw sir, that wasn't me," she said.

"Stop flirting with her," Gina snapped, "that pisses me off," she continued.

"I really don't want to do that," I said.

"Betsy, get back to work and stop jiving around," Gina said. I kissed Gina quickly on the cheek and she smiled.

We begin to playfully wrestle in bed. Then the smell of

eggs and bacon in the kitchen caught our attention and I turned on the television. "My vacation is over and I got to go to work today, but don't have to be in until ten o'clock," I said.

"You've been away most all the time. It's been a fun three weeks," she said.

"No, it's been a growing experience," I said.

"Well, sex is better than it ever was," she said.

"Betsy, Betsy," I yelled. She ran into the room.

"Yes sir," she said.

"Serve us breakfast in bed," I said.

"Coming up," she replied. As she walked out, Gina begins to fondle my crotch and it grew through my pajamas as Betsy returned with breakfast. Her face turned from pleasant to deep depression and I could see the contempt of Gina showing her who I belong too.

"Thanks Betsy," I said.

"We have so much laundry built up it's ashamed," Gina said.

"How did that happen you had some other guy over here while I was gone?" I asked, playfully.

"No way," exclaimed Gina.

"I have forgiven you, no matter what you did but there will be no second chance," I said.

"I didn't do anything," she said.

"Shut up and enjoy this before you open up an old wound," I snapped. But deep in my mind, I knew she was telling the truth but it's part of the leverage game of keeping her at bay. After we finished breakfast, I took a shower and got ready for work. I met Gina at the door as I was leaving.

"Goodbye honey," she said, and gave me a kiss. I waved her a goodbye with a big smile on my face thinking about the good sex we had last night.

I was sitting in my office chair thinking about the strange vacation I had. I grabbed a handful of papers that had accumulated in my basket and didn't know where to start. I logged onto my computer to pick up my E-mail when the phone rang. It was the CEO, he wanted to see me and have a cordial visit discussing my vacation. I was lost in how I would explain the whole situation I had encountered.

Meanwhile, Gina was taking a nice long bubble bath and Betsy sneaked into her room and was masturbating with a vibrator she had hidden in a drawer. She was lying across the bed and really getting into it and making loud moans and sounds of passion. Gina had just stepped out of the bath, dried herself off with a towel and walked through the kitchen to tell Betsy the bathroom laundry basket was full. There was no one in sight, so she walked to Betsy's room where one could hear the loudness of her lust emanating from the door. Gina barged in quickly to catch her in the act. "What the hell are you doing?" she snapped.

Betsy jumped up and sat up on the bed in embarrassment but she really didn't want to stop. "I am sorry Ma'am but I don't have a man," she said.

"That don't mean you can come over my house and do that shit," she barked. "I am so sick of you," she continued.

"I'm sorry Ma'am," Betsy begged.

"Get your ass dressed, go get washed off and get back to work," Gina said, disgustedly.

Betsy humbly walked to her bathroom with her head down in submission.

"Fifteen minutes," Gina said.

Later, Betsy was gathering laundry to wash and she saw a pair of my soiled underwear and she ran to her room to hide them away. She slipped it under her mattress and returned quickly to continued sorting clothes.

Gina was in the bedroom on the telephone talking to her sister. "So what's going on over there?" Lisa asked.

"Henry is back and we made real good love last night, the

best we ever had," she said.

"You better watch that maid of yours," Lisa said.

"Oh, you won't believe what I caught her doing today; I got out of the bath and was looking for her. But there wasn't a soul in sight so I walked down to her room and I could hear these loud sounds; when I opened the door she was inside playing with herself," she said.

"No, Ha Ha Ha," Lisa laughed,

"That nasty little freak," she continued. "Isn't she pathetic?" Gina said.

"What are you going to do?" Lisa asked.

"I don't know what to do, buy her a gigolo?" Gina joked.

"My home is fine, never any problems," Lisa said.

"But think about it, that nasty bitch masturbating," Gina said. "I have never seen a raccoon masturbate before," she laughed. "Nasty niger bitch," Gina said.

"Well, baby sister, I think I better get back to work," Lisa said.

"I forgot you got a job," she said.

"Everybody can't find a wealthy man to get with like you," Lisa said.

"We do OK but we are not rich," she said.

"Two brand new beautiful cars, a house close to being a mansion and you are not rich?" Lisa said. "Well," she said. "My boss is coming to check on me, bye," Lisa finished.

Gina hung up the phone and walked outside. It was a cloudy day that looked like it would start to rain at anytime. "I guess my roses won't need any watering today," she said.

Later that day, rain began to fall by the buckets and Miss Betsy had no way home. It was much too bad for her to go outside in the elements.

"You are not staying here tonight. Get your coat," Gina said, as she went to get her car keys.

"Thank you for the ride, Miss Gina."

"Shut the hell up, I don't feel like going out there myself," she snapped.

Betsy put on her coat and grabbed her belongings and they made a run for the car trying to stay as dry as possible. Gina cranked up the car and backed out. "Just remember, we don't have a damn thing to talk about on this ride. `Get it?'," she barked. With that she put the car in gear and they sped away.

Shortly after, Betsy was home and entered the door. "Who was that dropped you off?" Mama asked.

"Oh, that was that white girl," Betsy said.

"Yall getting along again?" Mama asked.

"No, she just didn't want me there when her husband got home," she said.

"Why she do that for? You got eyes for her husband?" Mama asked.

"No, Mama," she said. "I been drinking a little rum," Mama said, as she lifts up the bottle. "Do you care for a drink with your Mama?" she asked.

"Sure, what we mixing it with?" Betsy asked.

"What else, coke," she said, and laughed.

The phone rang and Betsy got up to get it. "Hello," she said.

"Girl, this is your cousin," Ida, said Ida. "I haven't found you a job yet but I am still looking," she continued.

"I sure may be needing one soon, the way that white girl is on my butt now days," she said.

"You ever drove a forklift," said Ida, jokingly.

"No, but I can learn if they give me the chance," she said.

"They are always looking for school bus drivers," Ida said.

"Girl, I'd be done killed one of those bad young ones," she said.

"I whoops mine," Ida said, "especially those bad ass little boys," she continued.

"I keep my little boys in line too, they know to pull those

pants down when I got the strap or they are going to get more," Betsy laughed. Her two twin boys heard it and looked at each other sadly, wishing they had a better mother where they could feel loved and not abused and treated like animals. "You ought to see how they looked at each other when I said that, Ida," she said.

"Mine that same way, they claim us grown people are abusing them. My three little girls, I don't have no problem out of, it's just those little boys. One claimed that a teacher liked his voice and he wanted to stay after school and sing," she said.

"He just wanted to get into some devilment," Betsy said.

"I told him, he better bring his ass in here after school is out and he bet not be late," she said.

"If you don't do that now, they'll be in jail when they get older and then they will be a worry to you," Betsy said.

"Then those old punks in jail will rape them and they wish they had listened to us. I got mothers' wit, a degree child, in it," Ida exclaimed.

"All those educated people think they know so much. They don't know a damn thing about nothing, they make all that good money and don't know shit," Betsy said.

"Sure you right," Ida said.

"Let me go; my Mama was making me a drink," Betsy said.

"OK, bye," said Ida.

Betsy hung up the phone and walked into the kitchen with her mother.

"For a minute, I was hoping you had found yourself a man but it wasn't enough laughter or shy question answering for it to be that," Mama said.

"No, Ma, I told you time and time again that don't no-good man won't me, they like those white girls. They drive around in those fancy cars, dressed all nice with a white girl beside them grinning from ear to ear. They don't want no sister," Betsy said.

"That's not all the way true, girl. There is a man for you somewhere," Mama said.

Betsy picks up her drink and sips. "Well, that's the way it's been for me," she says, and looks at her twin boys. "If they go get a white girl, they know not to bring her here in my house," she said. "And they ain't getting no college education through me, they going to go get a real man's job and use their hands for a living," she continued.

"Every man should use his hands," Mama said, "as long as he ain't using them for stealing," she continued.

Betsy gazed over at her girls who were watching television. "Look at them," she said, and pointed at them. "They so nice, quiet and well behaved," she said.

"They little girls right now, just wait," Mama said.

"I didn't cause you no problems, Mama," Betsy said.

"Your oldest sister did and that's why she's dead today. She was running after this no-good man, he had two girlfriends and his other woman shot my daughter." Mama weeps. "And she was only eighteen years old," she continued.

"Mama, don't cry," Betsy said.

"The girl was smart in school and make straight `A's' every time," Mama snapped tearfully.

Betsy walks over and gives her mother a hug. "Everything is going to be alright, Mama," she said.

CHAPTER EIGHT--Rocky Road

One week later, on a bright, sunny day, Gina and I were walking through the park. She saw the giant daffodils near the pond and was elated by their beauty. It was the first time she has felt deep joy since our two-week separation. "Those daffodils are so beautiful, I wonder if I could pick one and put in the large vase we have in our living room?" she said.

I didn't say anything. We walked over to a park bench and sat. She begins to rub on my thigh and I could feel my nature rise, and I kissed her as a summer breeze blew across our bodies. "Let's take this home," I said.

When we got home, Betsy was in the living room dusting, wearing spandex that showed her curves, with an apron on. "We didn't hire a damn french maid, go put something else on right now, goddamn it," Gina shouted.

"Baby, please don't yell," I said. She walked into the bedroom and came back with a bullwhip. "What the . . . ," I said, in shock.

Gina crack it across Betsy's back and she cried out.

"Oh no," I said, and grabbed the whip from Gina's hand. "What the hell is going on here? Betsy is not our slave and you don't have no business hitting her," I said. I walked over to Betsy and helped her to a chair. "You, take your ass in the bedroom and wait for me," I said.

"I'm sorry Betsy, please don't sue us. I will give you ten thousand in cash and you can keep the job," I said. She was still stunned from the pain. "Betsy, are you alright?" I reached in my pocket and began writing her a check. "Here take this; I will have a talk with my wife." I stormed into the bedroom with the whip. "Where the fuck did you get this?" I snapped, as I lifted the whip up. She cowered as I yelled. "Where damn it?" I barked.

"At a country western shop," she said.

"What would you do if I hit you with this?" I yelled.

She begins to cry. "I lost control of myself, and I was so upset that you were gone and I don't want to lose you again," she wept.

I threw the whip out the window. "We don't need that in our lives," I said, more softly.

I walked into the living room. "Betsy you can go home for today; hell take the rest of the week off. I'll still pay you in full," I said.

Betsy went into her room and got her stuff and left. I went into the bedroom and saw Gina sitting there looking very foolish. When she saw the disgusted expression on my face, she buried her face in a pillow in shame and began to cry.

"I ought to go get that whip and show you how it feels to be lashed across the back," I snapped.

As Betsy walked through her door she threw her things in a chair and went into the bathroom without speaking to anyone. "She must have had another bad day," Mama said. She pulled off her top and looked in the mirror, there was a welt on her shoulder, not breaking skin however.

Her mother called from the outside. "Betsy, I cooked your favorite meal: black-eyed peas, with ham hocks and corn bread, and rice pudding," she said.

Betsy pulled down her shirt and walked into the kitchen. "You're mighty quiet today. You want to talk about it?" she asked.

"I'm OK, just a little tired and hungry," she said and strained a grin.

"You sit right here and your Mama is going to fix you a plate just like I used to do when you were a little girl," she said.

Betsy's twin boys starting laughing but when she looked

at them they quickly stopped. She points at them. "Have they been giving you any trouble, Mama?" she asked.

"Naw baby, they been so sweet and precious," she said.

"Because if they have, I am going to blister their behinds and they won't be able to sit for a week," she said. The boys got up and went into the living room to watch television.

Her mother served her a plate and she ate sullenly. Later on that night, just when everyone was asleep. Betsy went into the twins room angry with a belt in her hand. "I seen where yall has been writing on the wall in the bathroom," she snapped. She pulled the quilts off the boys and began to beat them hard, on their backs, legs, and a few even landed on their face. She continued the beating and the sound of children cries echoed through the house. Her mother was fast asleep with her door locked and the twins had no one to intervene the severe beating that they were receiving.

She whipped those children on and on until her arm was tired. As she departed to her room, the boys were still weeping which turned to silent tears. "That'll teach you bad ass little boys, you got to learn how to obey a woman. Next thing you know, when you get grown yall be trying to marry a white woman," she snapped. She shook her head. "I don't think so, I'm going to fix that now. You are going to stick with your color. I am going to stay on you and make sure you do exactly what I want you to do," she continued.

Betsy went to bed with many things were running through her mind. She felt satisfied in her soul from whipping her children and letting out the anxiety in which her job had created inside. The thrill of abusing a man, although little boys, stimulated her sexually and she was very moist and excited. She got a vibrator from her drawer and inserted into her orifice and thought about the begging and pleading of her boys she had just punished. She stroked herself and the rhythm increased. Moans of joy filled the room until her body ruptured in climatic release. She silently went to sleep without washing the fluids from her fingers.

11am the next morning, Betsy was out doing some shopping pushing her cart down the aisle, when suddenly a lady in a short black skirt and a skimpy top which showed her attributes stopped her cart. "Hey, girl you remember me? It's been a long time," Tulip said.

Betsy took a step back and looked at her. "Hey," she said.

Tulip pulled her over to the side so no one could hear them. "I always loved you and you had to leave me for a man," Tulip said.

"My husband passed and I am all by myself," Betsy said.

"I still dance but I only do it in Las Vegas because it's more money there. Do you still take it off for the fellers?" Tulip asked.

"I gave that up after I got married and I got so many kids and stretch marks," she said.

"You still look good to me," said Tulip, as she looked down at her body and stopped at her buttocks.

"It gets cold sometimes in my bed," Betsy said.

"Mine too. I don't give a man the time of day but I'll do a little nude dance to get their money," she said.

"I wish I could say the same," Betsy said.

"Well, lets hookup and keep each other warm. I am still good," said Tulip.

"It would have to be over your place because my mother live with me and my kids," she said.

"Oh, that's no problem," Tulip said. She scrambled through her purse and wrote her name and number on a piece of paper and handed it to Betsy. "Call me anytime for any reason," she said.

Betsy took the piece of paper and slipped it into her pants. "I will be calling you," she said.

Tulip blew a kiss at her and walked out the door in a

slinky way.

Later, Betsy arrived home with clothes for her children. Her two little girls and her twins were watching with a sparkle in their eyes as she poured out the goods on the bed. She picked up a little dress and gave it to one of her girls and gave the other girl a little calico summer dress. "Yall go try that on and let me see how it fit," she said. They ran into their bedroom and changed clothes.

The two twin boys were looking as Betsy picked up dresses she had bought for herself. As their eyes roamed on the bed they could not distinguish anything that look like boys clothes. "Ain't no need in looking, I didn't yall bad ass shit," Betsy snapped.

The twins begin to whisper to each other and they left sadly. "Yall come back here," Betsy shouted and they returned with their heads down. "When yall stop drawing on the walls and stop laughing at silly things, I'll buy yall some stuff like your sisters," Betsy said.

The twins were not stupid enough to believe this. Even though they were very small they know when they hurt inside and they are being done wrong. Children sometimes have a great reasoning of what's right and wrong better than adults. They left again and they decided deeper in their hearts that they shared a sorry excuse for a mother no matter how hard she worked. Her efforts were not for them but for her own self purpose. They longed for their father and they became more silent, inward and would not smile at anyone. They were lost and unreachable except to each other. They would not speak to their sisters either.

The next day Betsy was lying across the bed talking on the phone. "Hello Tulip, this is Betsy," she said.

"Hey baby, what's going on? Do you want to come over tonight?" she asked.

"I am so horny I could almost die, I was thinking about the days when you used to do me good," she said.

"Well, I am going to get ready for bed and you come on over. I live at 1312 Oak drive and the door will be open. Do you want me to start without you or do you want me to wait?" she asked.

"Whatever you like as long as you have something for me," Betsy said. Then Betsy could hear the buzzing of a vibrator being turned on and Tulip moaned through the phone as she begins to play with herself. Betsy hung up the phone and hurriedly got dressed, her mother saw her.

"What's the rush baby?" she asked.

"Oh, I got to meet somebody," Betsy said.

"You got a man now? Why didn't you tell me about it? I wanted to asked you about the twins . . . they said the other night you spanked them," she asked.

"I got to go Mama, I am really in a hurry," she said, exited the front door and ran down the street. She waved down a taxi and paid him when they got to her destination.

She ran up to Tulips' door and eased inside. It was dark with a yellow light and you could hear soft moans coming out of the bedroom. Betsy locked the door, took off her coat, pants and top to bear her nude breast and pantied bottom. She then walked into the bedroom to see Tulip with her legs spread with a vibrator being inserted in and out of her womanhood. Tulip looked up with passion filled eyes. "I'm so glad you could make it, come here," she said and beckon her on to get into bed with her. Betsy took off her panties and got into bed with Tulip who took control of where her hands were doing the work. Betsy begins to slowly work the vibrator in and out. Tulip bucked wildly, hissed and moaned uncontrollably. Betsy begins to kiss her breasts as she worked on her. "Yes," Tulip replied.

Betsy kissed her deeply on her lips and they embraced for a moment as the vibrator laid motionlessly inside Tulip. "Tulip, spank me," Betsy pleaded.

"We have never did that before," Tulip said, but she removed the vibrator and put Betsy across her lap and began to spank her softly.

Betsy was not satisfied with the gentleness. "Beat me hard," Betsy cried.

Tulip began to spank her earnestly harder and harder as Betsy cried out in ecstasy. "Where did you begin to like this bitch?" Tulip barked.

"My boss spanked me once and I like it," she replied.

Tulip tossed her off and stood up to get a belt. "Get on your hands and knees on the bed," she said.

Betsy scrambled up into position and Tulip begins to whip her behind with the belt. "Count them off slut," she barks.

Betsy's mother was waiting for her return. "I hope my child is OK," she muttered to herself.

It was 5am and a car drove up and let Betsy out. Her mother was looking out the window but could not make out who was driving. When Betsy entered, her mother could tell she had been sexually relieved by her new glow that emanated. "Finally got you a man?" Mama asked.

"Not really," Betsy replied.

"I can feel the difference in you just as you stand there," Mama said.

Betsy walked out without much to say and went to bed. Her mother knew something was wrong but could not put a finger on it.

Meanwhile, Gina hadn't done a thing around the house and clothes were building up. There were dirty dishes in the sink and the bathroom was beginning to smell. Betsy was due to come back to work Monday. "Gina, could you clean up a little?" I asked. She was sullen that I had let Betsy off for the week but she also acknowledged it was her fault that all of this took place.

She moved very slowly to pick some things up and she did one load of laundry of attire that was necessary for us to continue living a hygienic life. "Gina, sit down," I said.

"I feel sick, in the morning I throw up," she said.

"I think maybe you need to go to the doctor," I said.

From the symptoms she gave the doctor, it sounded if though she was pregnant. She took a pregnancy test and the doctor said he will give us a call after the results are founded.

It was 7am Saturday and the phone rang. "Hello," Gina said.

"I would like to confirm to you that you are positively pregnant," the doctor said.

Gina hung up the phone in joy. "I finally did it," she shouted.

"Did what?" I asked.

"I am pregnant with your child," she replied, with a smile on her face. We hugged and kissed deeply.

"I love you," I said.

"I love you too," she said.

"Where you do want to go eat tonight?" I asked.

"I feel like eating lots of spaghetti," she replied.

"Pasta, it is," I said.   I started dancing around like a football player after he scores a touchdown. "Junior, junior, junior," I said.

Gina laughed at me. "You are so crazy but that's why I love you and you will always be mine," she said.

"I am going to call Betsy up and asked if she can come in tomorrow and straighten out this place. I will pay her a little extra," I said. I picked up the phone. "Hello, Betsy," I said.

"Hello," Betsy replied.

"Can you come in tomorrow and work? I will pay you a little extra. The house is a mess without you here and we just found out today that Gina is pregnant," I said.

"Sure," Betsy said, as her heart dropped knowing Gina was pregnant by me.

"Then everything is set?" I asked.

"Yes, Mr. Cook," she replied.

"The key will be under the mat because we not going to be here," I said.

"OK," Betsy said.

"Goodbye and have a nice day," I said. I turned around and ran to Gina and gave her a big hug. She laughed and was full of joy.

Later, we were eating spaghetti at a restaurant. "If it's a boy then we will name him after me," I said.

"What if it's a girl?" Gina asked.

"Then we will name her Gina junior," I said, playfully.

She laughed and reached for the wine.

"Nope, you can have none of that. I don't want no retarded children," I said.

"OK," she said.

"We can name the girl Gloria," I said.

"I like that," Gina said.

"Then that's what it will be," I said.

The waitress came over to our table. "Is everything here to your liking?" she asked.

"Get this girl some ice tea," I said.

"As you wish," she replied.

"I am getting tired of the people at work. I think I am going to open up a sports shop. I'll wait until it gets a good profitable start and then leave the company," I said.

"We have enough in the bank right now for that," Gina said.

"But I want to make sure because I don't want to fall flat

on my face and then not have a constant income coming in," I said.

"We have three million dollars in the bank," Gina replied.

"What? I didn't know I had that much in the bank," I said.

"We have been millionaires' for the past two years," Gina said.

"Then I think I will give them my resignation papers Monday," I said. "I would like to spend more time with you anyway and maybe golf a little bit more and enjoy my life," I continued.

"You are talking so much today," Gina said.

"I can't help it. You are holding our future in your womb; that's the most important thing to me," I said. She kissed me on the cheek. "Three million dollars in the bank?" I said.

Meanwhile, Betsy was with Tulip and they were drinking some white port wine and watching an all-girls action sex video. "Getting any new ideas?" Tulip asked.

Betsy shook her head.

"What's been eating you?" Tulip asked, as she ran her hand across Betsy's face. "You've been quiet all evening. You feel comfortable with me, don't you?" Tulip asked.

"I feel OK," Betsy replied.

"If you don't feel comfortable all you have to do is tell me," Tulip said.

"I will always love you," Betsy said.

"I love you too," Tulip said, and they kissed.

Deep inside Betsy was hurting at the thought of Gina being pregnant to a successful black man that was out of her reach. Betsy would much rather be with a man but Tulip was her only outlet.   Tulip could provide the passion and experienced touching that very few men could out do.

CHAPTER NINE--Betsy Rebukes

Sunday morning, Gina and I were in a hotel. I got up and turned on television. She was still asleep and lying on her side as I caressed her shoulder and gazed at her closely for one moment. My eyes affixed to her golden locks and slowly gazed upon her entire body very deeply noticing that she was everything that I envisioned in my mind as what I considered a perfectly beautiful woman. Her hands were small and fingers thin and feminine and soft to the touch as I gently held her hand. Her arms were slender and ladylike and not an area of fatty build up like I had seen in many black women when I was a boy. She sighed and rolled on her back and slightly opened her eyes and looked up at me and smiled beautiful as a new born baby.

"Did you sleep well?" I asked.

She inhaled and stretched her limbs; her body tightened up all over. "Yes, it was a good night's rest," she replied.

"Now I know why I married you," I said.

"Why?" she asked.

"Because you are beautiful inside and out," I said.

"Oh yea," she said and smiled.

I kissed her on the cheek and then got to her feet and tickled her. She laughed and tried to pull her legs away.

"Stop," she yelled.

I stopped and hugged her, kissed her on the ear and whispered softly with a breath of my exhalation: "I love you."

She laughed at me.

"What?" I asked.

"Nothing," she replied.

"No, really," I asked.

"I love you too," she said.

Meanwhile, Betsy had just arrived at our house and

looked under the doormat and got the key. She turned the key in the lock and opened the door. Her eyes were open wide as she walked through the house and saw the buildup of dirt, stains everywhere and dirty dishes in the kitchen sink. "Nasty white bitch," she shouted.

She didn't know where to start and she sat down to think for a minute. "They done nasty-up this house and called me to clean up their mess," she uttered. She went to get a broom. "No, I think I better pick everything up first and take out the trash," she said.

Later that afternoon Betsy's mother was sitting in a chair wondering why Betsy hadn't said anything about her night out. The phone rang and Mama answered. "Hello," she said.

There was heavy breathing and moaning, for it was Tulip masturbating in the background. "What the . . .," Mama said, in shock and hung up the phone. Minutes later Betsy came through the door and tossed her coat on the couch.

"Anybody call for me?" she asked.

"No baby," Mama replied.

"I'm tired," Betsy said.

"Well, go take a long, hot bath," Mama said.

"Oh, I don't have time; I'm going out tonight," she said.

"So, what's up with you? You got a man now?" Mama asked.

"I'm still looking," Betsy replied. After Betsy took a shower and got dressed she departed in a big hurry, without even as much as a goodbye to her mother.

"The girl is sprung," Mama said, "I hope he's a decent man," she continued.

Tulip was sitting at the bar when Betsy entered. Her eyes lit up as she caught her attention. "Damn, you look good tonight," said Tulip.

"I thought you said you were going to call me," Betsy asked.

"I did but whoever answered hung up," she replied.

"My Mama told me I didn't get any calls," Betsy said.

"Well, we are together now," Tulip replied, "besides what the sweat anyway. This is the 90's and everything is cool," she continued.

"I don't know," Betsy replied.

"You want a drink or do you want to go straight over my place?" Tulip asked.

Betsy hesitated for a moment. "Yes, let's go," she said.

When they departed many of the men inside watched Tulip twist out the door in a tight leather mini skirt. One of the men whistled. "Men, they are all pigs," she snapped.

Later as they laid in bed, spent from their sexual overtures, Tulip gently caresses Betsy's body. "I am so tired of working for this damn white bitch," Betsy said.

"If you quit, I'll take care of you," Tulip replied.

"I can't do that," Betsy said.

"Are you afraid of the pressure of being called gay?" Tulip asked.

"That's part of it, but," she said.

"That's OK," Tulip said.

"This white lady that I work for is married to this uncle Tom black man," she said.

"All black men are screwed up, all they want is for a woman to spread her legs. No matter what color she is," Tulip said.

"He really loves this girl," Betsy replied.

"Until she gets old," Tulip said. "That's why you're having problems finding one," she continued.

"Thirty-seven isn't old," Betsy snapped.

"But you have children. These men get you pregnant and then they run away," Tulip said.

"Tulip, my husband was a good man," she said.

"I didn't mean to get you worked up," Tulip said.

"I do understand where you are coming from," Betsy said.

Tulip embraces Betsy and kisses her deeply.

When Gina and I returned home later that night, the smell of pine oil, lemon and potpourri was all through the house and every room. The laundry was done and everything was in perfect place. "That Betsy, did it again," I said.

"It can't be all that clean," Gina said.

"Come on, let's go to bed and watch TV," I said.

We laid in bed watching the late movies until we both dosed off to sleep. Meanwhile, Betsy had just come into her house and her mother was waiting up for her. As Betsy closed the door and entered, "Sit down child, I want to talk to you," she said.

"What?" Betsy said, and sat down.

"You running around here and not telling anybody anything about nothing that you are doing. What is it that you are hiding? You forget but you my little girl and I know when you up to something you don't have no business," Mama said.

"Really, nothing, Ma," Betsy said, nervously.

"Well OK, if you say so," Mama said.

Betsy walked to her bedroom.

The next morning, Gina and I was up at 6am drinking coffee. "I am going to give the CEO my resignation papers today," I said.

"Are you sure you want to do that?" Gina asked.

"I've always wanted something of my own to have and now since we have a baby on the way, I would like to be home now and spend some quality time with you and build a business for myself," I said.

I went into the bedroom and got dressed for the final time to go to the office. I tied my shoes and made sure that my appearance was up to par. Gina walked into the bedroom as I was looking at myself through the mirror and hugged me from behind. "It's alot of women who would like to have a sexy older man like you," she said. I smiled as I combed my hair. It was 7:30am when I cranked my car. I could hear the school children's laughter as they walked down the street to school and the birds were singing in the trees. I backed out the driveway and burned rubber as I went down the street. Later, as Betsy walked through the door, Gina just looked at her with her hands on her hips and pouting. Betsy saw her demeanor and quietly went about her chores.

"Hey, you are not going to say, `Good morning' to me?" Gina barked.

"Sorry, Good morning, Miss Gina," Betsy said.

"That's better," Gina said, and went into the bedroom. "Niger bitch," Gina uttered.

Betsy walked into the bedroom. "I don't appreciate you hitting me with that bullwhip. I am not your slave," she said.

"Get out," Gina snapped.

"I'm not going to take any more shit off of you white bitch," Betsy shouted, and put her arms up like a boxer.

Gina screamed and charged her with anger and her arms flailing and Betsy stepped back and punched her in the jaw, Gina fell to the floor.

She got up quickly and ran up the stairs. "I'm going to shoot you bitch," Gina shouted.

After Betsy heard that she ran behind her to try to make it to the gun before she did. Gina lifted up the double shot gun and began to aim it as Betsy grabbed the barrel and it went off and fell off the balcony. "You gonna try to shot me bitch," Betsy barked. She grabbed Gina by the hair and punched her straight in the nose and sat on top of her.

"I am pregnant, you stupid niger," Gina shouted, as Betsy was on top of her. "I don't want to lose my baby," Gina cried.

When Betsy let her up, she swung wildly and missed and fell off the balcony. Betsy ran down the stairs to see if she were OK.

"Miss Gina," she said and shook her. Betsy felt for a pulse but there was none and blood was splattered all over the marble floor. Betsy begins to cry very loud. "Oh, what have I done?" she cried. Betsy quickly grasped hold of her emotions and knew that she would get the blame for killing Gina. No matter what she said. She quickly cleaned straightened up the house and went out in the backyard and dug a deep hole with a shovel. "I am sorry, Miss Gina, I didn't mean to hurt you bad," she cried, and dragged out Gina's dead body. "I hope the Lord will forgive me," she said.

She put the body in the hole and began to fill it with dirt. After she finished, she finished cleaning the remaining residuals of the struggle. "I am so sorry; I am sorry," she said, over and over. "I can call the police, but they won't understand and I have children to worry about," she cried. Betsy left and wrote a note. It read:

"Dear Mr. Cook,

I have to leave early today. I had an emergency at home and had to leave. Gina had left to the store and has not returned yet."

Betsy went into the bathroom and quickly took a shower and threw her clothes in the washer.

After she was done, she nervously walked out of the house to catch the bus.

When I arrive home later that day, I went through the house. "Gina," I yelled. I walked from room to room until I found the note and read it. "Oh, she just went to the store," I said.

I went into the bedroom and called Arnold but his girlfriend answered and said he was there.

Time went on, 7pm, 9pm, 12am, 3am and no sign of

Gina. I began to get worried and called Betsy's house; but she was not there. I stayed up until the 8am when Betsy was supposed to arrive but she called.

"Hello, Mr. Cook; I won't be in today," she said.

"Wait; Gina did not come home last night. Do you know what store she went to? I am worried sick," I asked.

"No, she didn't say," Betsy said.

"OK, thanks Betsy," I said, and hung up.

I put on my shoes and drove around going from store to store asking about her; but no one said they saw her. One day gone turned into two, then three, then a week. I was lost and deeply saddened for I had begun to believe she had ran out on me for good. I knew that she laughed when I told her that I loved her. I was beginning to think that the laugh was on me.

As weeks grew longer and stayed recluse, Betsy and I began to grow more fond of each other. One day as I was relaxed in a chair drinking a beer. Betsy caught me at the right moment and she came out of her bedroom wearing spandex that fitted her buttocks very tight. I asked her to come to me and she sheepishly sat on my lap and I begun to caress her thighs and my penis grew underneath her. "Let's go to the bedroom," I said.

She started to take off her top and I slapped her on the buttocks. "You like that, don't you?" I asked.

"Yes," she said.

I pushed her on the bed on her back and she smiled. She knew I was very horny and the alcohol had taken it's effect on my judgement. After a long night of sex, I was awakened to the smell of bacon and eggs. I was still nude. I got up quickly and wrapped myself in a robe. I had only vague memories of what happened in my bedroom and it seems like it was only a dream. When I walked into the kitchen, Betsy was moving about happy as a lark and singing as she prepared breakfast. "Betsy, I didn't do anything with you last night; did I?" I asked.

"You don't remember?" she asked.

"No, tell me what happened," I asked.

"We just made love all night until you went to sleep. Maybe three times," she said.

"I want you to act like this never happened," I snapped.

"Why, it was natural," she said.

"I'm married," I said.

"Oh, she probably left town with another man. How long has it been now since we heard from her?" she asked.

"Maybe she has but I don't know that for sure and if you do anything to hurt me and my wife's relationship, you are out of here," I snapped.

"Yes sir," she replied.

Meanwhile, Tulip was worried sick and wondered what had happened to Betsy and called her on the phone. "Hello," Mama answered.

"Is Betsy there?" Tulip asked.

"No, she isn't, may I ask whose calling?" Mama asked.

"Tell her Tulip called," she replied.

"OK," Mama said, she hung up the phone.

Later that evening Betsy returned home and in the living room the children were watching cartoons and laughing. Her mother was knitting a sweater and humming a gospel tune and rocking in a rocking chair. "Hi, Mama," she said.

"Someone called for you today," she said.

"Who?" Betsy asked.

"Oh, it was a lady," Mama replied.

"Did she leave a message?" Betsy asked.

"No, just seemed kind of upset," Mama replied.

Betsy looked at the twins. "There those two bad boys," she snapped.

"Girl, you ain't been the same in weeks. First you go out at night and stay and now since Gina is missing, I don't hardly see you at all," Mama said.

"Mr. Cook needs me more around the house now," Betsy replied.

"Is that all?" Mama asked.

"Well, I think that white woman ran off with Michael tell the truth and Mr. Cook can soon be considered a single man," Betsy said.

Her mother didn't say anything and walked into her bedroom and started to pray very loud to God.

Betsy went into her room and changed clothes and walked down the street. Tulips' car was parked and waiting for her on the street corner. Betsy got inside the car and Tulip slapped her. "I've been worried sick over you bitch," she barked.

Betsy begins to whimper and Tulip caresses her cheek where she had just slapped her. "I am sorry, she said, softly." She started up the car and drove away.

Betsy's mother saw her get into the car out of her window. "I wonder what my daughter doing?" she said.

When Tulip and Betsy arrived at there place, Tulip kissed Betsy on the neck and begin to gently caress her buttock as they stood in the living room. Tulip started to unbutton Betsy's shirt and caress her breast and they begin to slowly journey into the bedroom.

"Take off everything," Tulip said.

Betsy begins to take off her clothes and Tulip opened her dresser drawer and got out a long vibrator and turned it on. The hum of the device was loud and the sounds of passion echoed through the house. Later they are in the Iacuzzi bath playing with the bubbles and laughing.

"I stayed awake all night drinking whiskey and worrying about Gina. I could not believe that she would leave me like this without even a dear john letter." I sat and thought about it over and over again wondering what happened when everything seems to be shaping up so well. Was she really pregnant by me? I asked myself but I knew the chances were very slim as I carefully analyzed the situation and came to conclusion that was not it or at least as I logically deducted the circumstances. I poured myself another drink and another until I passed out in a living room recliner. I awaked the next morning with the sun in the window shining in my face, blinding me by its brightness. I was still drunk and I took an early morning drink and went into the bathroom and washed my face. I heard the door open and I knew it was Betsy coming to take care of the house. Betsy walked through the house humming and singing. I could tell by her joyous demeanor and she walked down the hall close to the bathroom.

"Good morning, Mr. Cook," she said.

"Not to me," I replied.

"It'll get better with time," she said.

"Have you found you a man yet?" I asked.

"I am still looking but it sure is alot of fun shopping," she replied.

The word shopping made me turn sobber because that was the last thing Gina was supposed to be doing before she disappeared. I walked out of the bathroom in a sullen way and didn't say anything else all day and just continued to drink my whiskey. In my mind many words were going around in my head. "Dear Gina, I miss you so, I never knew how much more I truly love you until this time came where I imagine in my mind I may never touch you again and you are probably in another man's arms but how, I asked because no one really loves you like I, deeply, truly and with the essence of my being and the innocence I protected from all mankind and the cruelty of life to give to you unblemished and untouched as sweet of a love as only a virgin girl possess. Like this I love thee with all my heart and soul."

CHAPTER TEN--Maid to kill

I was awakened to the sounds of dogs fighting in my backyard. I didn't know what was going on but I hoped that it would soon stop. My head was really ticking from all the liquor I had consumed the last couple of days. I looked up at the clock; it was three o'clock in the morning. There was no way I was going to go outside to find out what the dogs were up to. I knew I didn't own a dog and wondered how they got into my yard before I dozed back off to sleep. When I awoke again four hours later, I found myself wet where I had pissed on myself. The bed was soaked with it and the central heat made the smell of it drying emanate all through the house. I got up and let up a few windows and I could smell the odor of something rotten like an unclean trash can but it was not trash day. I put on my jogging suit and took a walk in the neighborhood. I heard the birds singing in the formosa tree across the street. The squirrels were looking for pecans at the house on the corner. The sun had just begin to break through to clouds to warm the atmosphere to comfort. I looked at my watch and it was 6:45am.

I walked to the park and sat on a park bench and just threw rocks into the pond. The geese were walking about the ground trying to get the earthworms that may have surfaced or bugs that were crawling. I was thinking about how I resigned and told my CEO how I wanted to spend more time with my wife. Now I have neither job nor wife but I have three million dollars in the bank and a lonely house with a horny maid.

I looked down at my tennis shoe and noticed it was untied and as I leaned forward to tied them up all the vertebrates in my back cracked. I looked up into the sky after I tied my shoe and saw a small plane fly over. I begin to think about taking a trip somewhere, maybe Las Vegas or New York.

It was 8am now and Betsy had just walked through the door and there was silence all about the house. She went about her regular routine then she smelled a rancid odor that was strong. She went outside into the backyard and noticed that the dogs were digging up the body she had buried. She quickly went into the garage and got a shovel to replace dirt the dog had taken out of the hole. The arm of the body was now exposed and there were flies all around its hatching larva worms that ate festively. Betsy worked hard and fast to cover the body with dirt because she didn't know at what time I would return. When I walked through the door Betsy had just came in from the backyard and her dress was covered with dirt. "How you get so dirty?" I asked.

"I was just tending to the bushes in the back," she replied.

"You don't have to do that. I hired you only for housework," I replied.

"It's no bother, I kinda like to get out of the house once and a while," she replied.

"I have been lost ever since Gina been gone," I said.

"She probably partying somewhere right this moment," Betsy said.

"She's pregnant, how much partying can she do?" I asked.

"Well, I was just trying to make you feel better and all you do is drink now. I am going to cook you some pancakes this morning," she said.

"I think you better clean that dirt off of you first," I said.

"Oh yea," she said, and went to the bathroom.

I took a bottle of whiskey out of the bar and went outside on the front porch and sat with a glass and began to pour me a drink. "I ain't letting no bitch tell me when I can drink," I uttered. "That bitch ain't lost nobody," I continued as I poured myself a drink.

Betsy came outside on the porch after she had cleaned up.

"Mr. Cook, I hate what you are doing to yourself," she said.

"You have not lost anybody," I barked.

"I lost my husband not too long ago, but I got over it and I didn't drink when I was missing him," she said.

"I don't have any children and Gina was pregnant when she left," I said.

"You don't know if she was pregnant by you or somebody else," Betsy replied.

"Well, it's none of your goddamn business anyway, now get your ass back in the house and clean like I pay you to do," I snapped.

She went back inside and slammed the door.

"I don't give a shit about you slamming the door," I shouted.

She shortly returned. "You ever thought about getting with a sister?" she asked.

"Not recently, I am still married," I replied.

She giggled ignorantly and went back inside. "I am about to get me a new husband, a successful one, a millionaire," she uttered. She picked up the telephone and called Tulip.

"Hello," Tulip replied.

"This is Betsy, it's over with for us," she said, and hung up the telephone.

"Wait, wait," Tulip replied. Tulip was in an anger tantrum and she called Betsy's house and her mother answered.

"Hello," Mama said.

"This is Tulip. I dare you to tell me I can no longer see your daughter. We've been friends for a long time and lovers too," she cried.

Mamas' mouth dropped and she fell into a chair. "Say what?" she asked.

"I know you object to her seeing another woman but I love her," Tulip continued.

"I didn't no nothing about this," Mama replied.

Tulip hung up the telephone. "That will teach her for being ashamed of being gay," she snapped.

Betsy's mother was in shock. "Oh, my God have mercy," she cried.

Later that night when Betsy came home her mother was waiting for her at the door. "I heard why you been out all nights without an explanation. Yes, your lover called here upset you left her," Mama said.

"I can explain Mama," Betsy said.

"You don't have nothing to say to me, hiding around and sneaking around at night," she snapped.

"Oh Mama, I'm sorry," Betsy said.

"Leave me alone, I am going to bed," Mama said.

Betsy felt rejected and unloved by her mother so she went into her bedroom and wept. "I am so confused," Betsy cried.

I was taking off my clothes getting ready for bed when the dogs begin to fight in the backyard again. I wasn't as drunk as I was the night before so I took a look out the window. They were digging something up and they were fighting and barking. When I opened the back door, a terrible stench assaulted my nostrils. "Oh my, God," I said.

I closed the door and went back inside. I was wondering what in the hell was buried that could be smelling like that. Maybe a dog had died fighting the other dogs, I thought but I was going to take a look in the morning. I closed all the windows and turned my thermostat to 60 degrees and went to bed. The full moon shone through my window as I gazed up into the stars and the darkness that surrounded them until I could marvel no more. My eyelids closed from my weariness into a deep, sound sleep.

I awoke at 6:45am the next morning. As I went outside to get my morning paper, I could still hear the dogs in my backyard growling and making alot of noise. I walked through the garage and shouted. The dogs ran. I held my breath and walked up to the area they were digging and I could see a human arm and a hand that had a ring on it. I looked at it closely and I recognized it was Gina's.

I fell to the ground on my knees and begin to cry uncontrollably. Finally when I gathered myself I called the police. When they arrived I pointed to where I found Gina's body and a homicide detective came up to me.

"Hello sir. I am lieutenant Jackson," he said and we shook hands. "When was the last time you saw your wife?" he asked.

"Maybe three or four weeks ago," I replied.

"Who was the last person to see her alive that you know of?" he asked.

"My maid," I replied.

"What time will she be in?" he asked.

I looked at my clock and it was 7:30am. "In about another 30 minutes," I replied.

Jackson pointed at another officer and told him to park at the corner up the block and told another officer to park a block up in the other direction.

"What type of car does she drive?" Jackson asked.

"She rides the bus," I replied.

"Did she have any fights with your wife, bad words exchanged or anything of that nature?" he asked.

"Well, sort of but nothing very serious," I replied.

Betsy was walking down the street. As she approached closer, she could see the police cars. When she got within three houses of mine she begins to run but a squad car pulled up to her and put her inside then drove her to my place. The officer got out of the car and opened the back door to let Betsy out and led her up to lieutenant Jackson. "She started to run when she saw the police cars," the officer said.

Betsy was looking down.

"We found Gina's body in the backyard," Jackson said, "would you know anything about that Betsy?" he asked.

"I killed her sir, but it was an accident and I knew no one would believe me," she said.

"You have the right to remain silent, anything you say can be used against you in a court of law," Jackson said.

As they took her away, she turned around and looked at me. "I love you, will you wait for me when I get out of jail?" she said.

I turned my back.

"I love you, wait for me," she shouted at me. "I will kill you too, you white girl loving bitch," she shouted.

I turned and looked at her in disbelief with my mouth open in shock.

"Please, marry me when I get out," she shouted.

I went back into the house and began to cry. I reflected back into my past life from my childhood and all the way into my adult life. My mother was a cruel, abusive, and uneducated black woman but was kind and loving to her white boss' children. All the black women that I met all my life had done some wrong doing to me and even when I left them alone and married a beautiful white female, the black woman kills her and they will probably feel vindication from this. Me, the nerd they laughed at in school and no one would have anything to do with because I am an intelligent black man. I broke an unwritten law of black people. If you are a black man, all black women are smarter than you and you are dumb. I don't have a right to be intelligent and be a black man. To seek success and be independent and financial liberated from the death grips of poverty. In the end of it all a man must be a man and stand on his feet not being a beggar who whine when he crawls for pennies.

About the Author

Gregory Walker was born on February 8, 1961, in Dallas, Texas. He had his first book contract offer when he was a junior at Roosevelt High School in Dallas. He joined the Navy following his graduation from high school and has been published in many small newspapers in the Seattle area and had his first poetry book, *The Inspired Life*, published in 1987.

In addition to his first novel, *Maid to Kill*, he has a screenplay being edited, *Meka and Alexander,* and his second book of poetry, *Twenty-Five Years of Poetry*, will be submitted for publication soon. He also possesses a beautiful singing voice and will be in the recording studio to complete his first single early in the year 2000.